UP
FOR
GRABS

We acknowledge financial support for our publishing activities: the
Government of Canada, through the Canada Book Fund and The Canada Council
for the Arts; the Government of Ontario, through the Ontario Arts Council,
Ontario Creates, and the Ontario Book Publishing Tax Credit. We acknowledge
additional funding provided by the Government of Ontario and the Ontario Arts
Council to address the adverse effects of the novel coronavirus pandemic.

Library and Archives Canada Cataloguing in Publication

Title: Up for grabs / Michelle Mulder.
Names: Mulder, Michelle, (Author of Out of the box), author.
Identifiers: Canadiana (print) 20230140858 | Canadiana (ebook) 20230140866 |
ISBN 9781770866942 (softcover) | ISBN 9781770866959 (HTML)
Classification: LCC PS8626.U435 U6 2023 | DDC jC813/.6—dc23

United States Library of Congress Control Number: 2023930221

Cover art: Julie McLaughlin
Interior text design: Marijke Friesen
Manufactured by Houghton Boston in Saskatoon,
Saskatchewan in February, 2023.

Printed using paper from a responsible and sustainable resource,
including a mix of virgin fibres and recycled materials.

Printed and bound in Canada.

DCB Young Readers
An imprint of Cormorant Books Inc.
260 Ishpadinaa (Spadina) Avenue, Suite 502, Tkaronto (Toronto), ON M5T 2E4
www.dcbyoungreaders.com
www.cormorantbooks.com

UP
FOR
GRABS

MICHELLE MULDER

Chapter One
July 2015

Zac was never big on talking about family, but you'd have thought a detail like "Grandma lives in a mansion with a castle outside her kitchen window" might have come up at some point. A castle. With turrets, a covered carriageway, and big lawns. Sure, a big ring of houses surrounded it now, but who knew Canada's west coast even *had* a castle?

Our grandmother's front porch was huge, and the house was up on a slope, so you had to clomp down the wooden steps to the stone ones before finally reaching the pavement.

We'd been here for a week now, and we hadn't met anyone — unless you could count the woman halfway down the street who was always sitting on her porch. She waved at me every time I went by. I waved back, but we never said a word to each other. She was the only person I ever saw outside. The only light I ever saw in a window was in the house across the street. A kid my age lived there with his mom. No one else ever seemed to be home anywhere on our street. *That's the trade-off,* Zac said when I mentioned it to him. *Living here means you have a big house near a castle, but you work so hard that you never have time to enjoy it. I'd rather have small and comfy any day.*

As far as I was concerned, they could all keep their castle. For me, the best part of the neighborhood was the tiniest house, which stood on a post at the edge of someone's property at the end of the street. The little box was an exact copy (just a billion times smaller) of the house under renovation behind it. I unhitched the latch at the side and pulled open the door to peer at the two neat rows of books.

"Hey, Pierre," I said. "The romances with the cringe-worthy covers are still here. They haven't moved all week."

Pierre pushed his silver hair back from his face. You'd never guess he was in his seventies. He looked like he split his time between the gym and the tanning salon, although he never set foot in either. "Someone has taken the pot roast cookbook." He snapped his fingers like he was disappointed that it had gotten away. "*Suburban Haiku* is new, though, no?"

"Hi, Pierre!" said a voice from behind us. I turned to see a boy about my age crouched a few feet away, opening a green backpack and smiling up at us. A notepad and a pen stuck out from the back pocket of his jeans, and I, as someone who carries a sketchbook and a pencil everywhere I go, appreciated that detail.

"Hazeem!" Pierre said. "It is a pleasure to see you again. This is my young friend, Frida. The one I was telling you about." Thankfully, he didn't add all the details that my brother Zac usually added at this point: that I was named after Frida Kahlo, a Mexican artist last century who was into bright colors and was way ahead of her time. Mom was a fan, and so was I for that matter, but no way was I going to mention this to a kid I'd just met, even if Hazeem *did* keep a notepad and a pen in his back pocket.

"I've seen you sitting on the front steps," Hazeem said, "drawing or writing or something. I live across the street. For the summer, anyway. We're from the Yukon."

"We're here for the summer too," I said.

"I know," Hazeem said. "Pierre told me. I met him last week when he got here. He said that he wasn't living at the house, just opening it up to air it out, but that someone my age would be arriving soon to stay for the summer."

I eyed the notepad in his pocket. "Do you sketch too?"

He shook his head. "I write."

"Hazeem is working on a story about the Munich Olympics crisis," Pierre said, as though everyone knew what that was (I didn't) and as though Hazeem wouldn't mind him mentioning this quirky interest to another teenager.

Hazeem didn't look embarrassed, though. "I was asking Pierre if he remembered any details."

Pierre closed the door of the box. "Nothing for me today, although the *Book of Knots* is tempting. I will say goodbye now to the two of you. I need to run a few errands and then I will go back to my boat. I think the problem with the propeller may be barnacles."

"Barnacles?" I asked. Pierre hadn't been planning to be in Victoria when we got here, but he was in the area and the propeller of the sailboat he lived on was doing some strange things so he was mooring here for a bit to investigate.

"They are getting in the way of the spinning," he said. "Today, I will try to scrape them off."

"Sounds like you have quite the afternoon ahead of you," I teased.

"Indeed!" he said. "Hazeem, it was a pleasure. Frida, I will see you and Zac again tomorrow."

Pierre headed off down the street. I was turning in the opposite direction, but Hazeem kept talking. "Liz keeps this box well-stocked." He jerked his head at the house surrounded by scaffolding. A few dumpsters stood in the driveway, and roof shingles speckled the pavement. He opened the book box and began sliding paperbacks onto the shelves. At his feet, his backpack stood open, brimming with more books. "What do you like to read?"

"Art books, mostly," I said, "but I'll read almost anything. Except romances and 1960s cookbooks."

"Good call," he said. "You should check out the box at Langham Court Theatre. I always see art books in there."

"There's another book box like this?" I asked. "Is it far from here?"

He shook his head. "Just a few blocks. I can show you, if you want. I don't think all these books will fit in here anyway, so I planned on a walk. Liz here printed a map for me of all the local book boxes — the ones in the neighborhood, anyway, not all three hundred."

"*Three hundred?!*"

Whatever expression I had on — excitement? admiration? — totally shifted the conversation. Hazeem's face lit up. "Isn't it fantastic? Sometimes I spread the books around a bit, like if one box gets too crowded and another is half-empty, you know? That's how I know the Langham Court Theatre one almost always has art books."

It was the nerdiest thing he could possibly say, and either he didn't know, or he didn't care. I felt myself relax. "What are some of the best titles you've seen so far?"

"*God Is Not a Fish Inspector*," he answered without even having to think about it. "It was a book of short stories or something."

"Excellent." I hesitated, wondering if I should add that to the list of weird titles that I'd started at the back of my sketchbook, but decided I should only include ones I'd seen myself. "My favorite so far is *The Curtain Book: A Sourcebook for Distinctive Curtains, Drapes, and Shades for Your Home.* That was here until Tuesday. I bet there are tons of really random books out there. I'd like to see that map sometime." I looked down at his backpack. "Did these all come from other boxes?"

"Nah," he said. "I'm helping a neighbor clear out her shelves. She's eighty-three. They're mostly about local history, but they're kind of historic themselves. They all end about fifty years ago."

That sounded familiar. Zac and I had been neck-deep in historic stuff ever since we got here. "The house we're in, it was my grandmother's. She died a few months ago, and —"

"I'm sorry," Hazeem said. "My grandfather died last year. I know how rough it is."

I bit my lip. "Actually, I barely knew her. I mean, I wish I did, but she didn't — she was kind of —"

"Oh," he said.

We stood there awkwardly while I tried to figure out what to say next. I'd had friends who'd lost grandparents, and friends whose parents had divorced, and Zac always told me to talk about it right away, say how sorry I was, and let the other person lead the conversation. Great advice, if I could avoid thinking about what life would look like if *I* lost anyone because the only Anyone I had was Zac. Sure, we saw Pierre every few years, and he was a great guy, but basically, it was Zac and me. If Zac kicked the bucket, I was on my own, and that's not something I ever wanted to think about. "I'm sorry about your grandfather. Sounds like you were close."

Hazeem nodded. "*Dada* — that's grandfather in Urdu — lived in Pakistan. That's where he died, but he spent every summer with us. This is our first one without him. That's part of why we came to Victoria." His eyes looked sad, but he talked like it was the most normal thing in the world to be standing on the sidewalk telling a complete stranger how much he missed his dead grandfather. Part of me wanted to turn and run, but a part of me was fascinated. What else would he talk about as if it was a totally normal conversation topic?

The click of high heels on pavement hurried toward us. A woman dressed like she was ready for the office rounded the hedge and stopped short, her mass of silver, wiry curls bobbing. She had a handbag big enough to put Mary Poppins to shame. "Good morning, Hazeem," she said.

"Hi, Liz," he said. "Have you met Frida? She's here for the summer."

"Pleased to meet you," I said.

"Are you staying at Anna's too?" Liz asked.

I shook my head. "At the house across the street from Hazeem's."

"Ooh! Such a lovely property!" Liz lied. (The place hadn't seen paint in decades and some of the windows didn't close properly. Inside, every nook and cranny was crammed with stuff, and everything reeked of mothballs.) "So much potential, and such a shame about the lady of the house. A relative of yours perhaps?"

I glanced at Hazeem to see if this line of conversation felt a bit intense to him too. He shrugged. "Liz works for an auction house. She's always on the lookout for —"

"Opportunities to help people choose mindfully between the possessions they'd like to keep and the ones that would fetch an excellent price in our showroom. Here —" She plunged a hand deep into her bag and pulled out a business card. "My contact information. I'm happy to help any time. I offer free consultations, of course."

Pushy much? "Thank you."

I slid the card into the back pocket of my cut-offs, and she trained her eyes on Hazeem. "How are things going at Anna's house? Anything she'll need help with?"

He shook his head. "Not so far. It's mostly papers and books she's getting rid of. Lots and lots of books."

"Well, you've got my number if you need me," Liz said. "Or just knock. You know I'm in the cottage at the back while the renos are going on, right? Oh my! Look at the time! I'm running late. Nice to meet you, Frances! Toodle-oo!" She clicketty-clicked down the street to a yellow Smart car, squeezed in, and took off.

"Frances!" I said.

Hazeem was laughing. "I thought it was only *my* name she got wrong — Hakim, Joaquin, Hansel, Hiram, Hazmat, Hoser —"

"Hoser?"

"Just kidding," he said. "It didn't get *that* bad, but it was bad enough for Anna to make her write my name ten times so she would remember it."

"I like this Anna person," I said. "How do you know so many people on the street already, anyway? How long have you been here?"

Hazeem shrugged. "A few weeks. Anna's our landlady and our neighbor too. Liz keeps showing up because she heard Anna's getting rid of stuff. Other than Pierre, Anna, and Liz, we don't know anyone. People don't seem to talk to each other much around here, you know? There's a neighborhood barbecue next week, though. You probably have a flyer in your mailbox."

"I'll look for it," I said.

He zipped up his backpack. "Right. This box is full, so next stop, Langham Court. Wanna come? It's only about five blocks from here. I guarantee art books, or double your money back."

"Such a deal!" I said. "You're on."

A few minutes later, we were standing in front of a tall cupboard with four shelves crammed to overflowing with everything from chewed-on board books to ancient copies of Shakespeare. "Look at that!" I pulled out a book called *30,000 Years of Art: The Story of Human Creativity across Time & Space.*

"Jackpot," Hazeem said. "I knew you'd find something. And what about this one? It's about a photographer, someone called Hannah Maynard who lived here in the late 1800s. That counts as art, right? Wanna read it?"

I wasn't much into photography, but Zac said our grandmother's house was built in 1911, and I did wonder what Victoria looked like back then. "Thanks."

By the time we were ready to leave, Hazeem had emptied his backpack, and I'd filled it with books I wanted to take home. One was so big that I had to carry it in my arms.

"Thanks for making space at the book exchange," Hazeem teased. "I couldn't have fit in Anna's books without you."

"Any time," I said. "Wouldn't this be easier by bike, though?"

"Don't have one," he said.

"I might be able to fix that." I told him about the old bike I'd spotted in our grandmother's basement. "It needs new inner tubes and the chain needs grease, but I can get it working. We'll have to fix it up for Zac to sell it anyway. You could borrow it in the meantime."

"Perfect," Hazeem said. "You look after the bikes. I'll map out some routes."

I smiled. This fancy, empty neighborhood wasn't a place I'd ever imagined living. Usually, we arrived somewhere with a long list of things to see or experience, but here, the list had been mind-numbingly short: sort and sell all of grandmother's stuff, including the house. It was a relief to add "treasure hunt with interesting new neighbor" to the list. "Book boxes of Victoria, here we come!"

Chapter Two

My brother was elbow-deep in a box of faded towels. He pulled one out, sneezed, and tossed it onto a growing pile. "There *has* to be a better way."

"To sort towels?" I asked. "If you —"

"No," said Zac, "to make enough money to retire by age thirty and travel until the end of time." That had been my brother's dream for as long as I could remember, but it had always been more of a joke than a real possibility. That's what I'd thought, anyway, until we inherited our grandmother's house and everything in it — over a hundred years' worth of my family's junk. (We'd been sorting for days already. Zac insisted on taking a picture of every single item and uploading it to see how much people charged for similar things online. That morning, he'd been snapping pics of a box of paperclips. *Hey, they could be vintage!* Sheesh.)

"You know that huge book on conceptual art that Hazeem found for me?" I asked. "Okay, okay. Wipe that smirk off your face, Dad-ee-o. So I've been talking about it a lot. It's a good book. You ever heard of Piero Manzoni?"

"If you keep calling me Dad-ee-o, little sister," Zac said, "I'll stick my fingers in my ears so I *can't* hear about him."

"Real mature," I said, but I was laughing.

"Speak, Young Person." He flattened the now-empty towel box and tossed it onto an armchair, the only surface that wasn't yet covered with piles of magazines, china plates, random knickknacks, or other junk. "Tell me about Piero Manzoni."

"Italian artist, 1960s, already super-famous by the time he was twenty-eight," I said. "Whatever he made, people would buy for a ridiculous price, and he hated that, so —"

Zac looked up from a stack of magazines. "An artist who hated making money?"

"He wanted people to pay attention to the art, not the artist," I said. "So he did a project that made his point: he sold his own poo for the price of its weight in gold!"

"*What*!?" Zac stood up, bashing into the mangy moose head hanging on the wall. He swore — my brother, not the moose — and rubbed the back of his head. "He sold his own poo? Why didn't *that* ever occur to me?"

"Crazy, right? So he made these ninety cans of poo —"

"Wait," Zac said. "Ninety? And he *canned* it?"

"Yeah, they look like little tuna cans, all sealed, with a label in four languages. A number on each can."

Zac shook his head. I loved telling him these stories. We'd gone all over the world, visiting art galleries wherever we could, and conceptual art like this always made him cringe. I kept telling him it wasn't about beauty. It was about making people think. He said it took no skill. (Once, we saw a poster at a museum that was super famous. The artist had hand-written *I will not make any more boring art* over and over again all the way down the page. No skill, Zac said. Hilarious and ironic, I said.) Adults can get a bit stuck in their ways. Someday, he'd thank me. "The best part about the cans," I said, "is that no one knows what's *actually* inside. If you open a tin, it's worthless. Half a million dollars down the drain."

"Down the toilet, so to speak," said Zac.

"Har, har."

"Now if I had a mind like that poo guy, what would I do with all this?" He waved a hand at the antiques, china plates, and thick, dusty drapes.

"Sell it as art." I put a folded towel on my hand, raised it toward the ceiling, and pouted like models do in fashion magazines. "Ees bee-you-ti-ful, *non*?"

"Ees very bee-you-ti-ful, *ma cherie*," Zac agreed, "and eef you can get an arteest's price for zat towel, I'll take you to any art museum your 'eart desires."

"Meh." I tossed the towel back onto its heap. "You have to be famous to get away with stuff like that. The art world doesn't take thirteen-year-olds seriously."

"Good thing thirteen doesn't last forever, eh?" Zac said. "Before you start digging through that box, do you mind clearing off the desk in the corner?"

I turned to the piles of old bills and flyers and unearthed some postcards. "These are from us!" The top ones were from our most recent trips to Belize and St. Kitts, but deeper in the pile, I found cards we'd written from France and even as far back as Argentina. "This one's from 2005. I was three. Did she keep all of them?"

"Looks like she never threw anything out," Zac said, "but don't go thinking she was sentimental. She never was."

"No kidding." Sentimental types probably talk to their grandkids sometimes. Apparently, even when Zac and I lived in the upstairs apartment when I was little, she barely spoke to us. When we moved out — because Zac had always wanted to travel, and he found a job in Argentina as a nanny, so he could look after me at the same time — our grandmother stopped talking to us altogether. We wrote postcards, and Zac called, but she didn't answer the phone often, and she never called back. Zac never talked about her much, but when he did, he always said something like *You can pick your nose, but you can't pick your family.* "Hey, did I tell you I met someone who works at an auction house? She was a bit creepy, like everywhere she looked, she saw dollar signs, but you know how to handle people like that, and maybe she could help us sell some of this stuff."

"I wouldn't let her anywhere near it," said Zac. "Auction houses take a huge cut. Besides, we still have to go through everything anyway. I've lost count of how many ten-dollar bills I've found hidden in weird places. Did she not believe in banks, or what?"

I was quiet for a moment. It was weird getting to know someone only through the objects she left behind (and where she stuffed her money). "What about the castle? Wouldn't a museum want some of these antiques?"

"I hadn't thought of that. Worth asking. I'll make a note." Zac patted down his pockets. "Now where did I put my phone?"

"On the box of Christmas decorations. Under the horrendously ugly wall clock in the kitchen."

"Er-hem, that's five hundred dollars' worth of ugly, I'll have you know. If it's an authentic mid-century starburst atomic wall clock — and I think it is — it'll buy us weeks of groceries." He picked his way across the room, squeezing between furniture and boxes, and disappeared into the kitchen.

I slipped our postcards into my sketchbook. I knew Zac didn't want me collecting stuff. Our own house was tiny, and he didn't believe in spending money on storage (or on anything other than food and traveling, to be honest). He probably wouldn't have cared about a few postcards, but it was simpler not to ask.

"This place used to be even more cramped, you know." He tucked his phone into his pocket. "You couldn't even see the walls when I was growing up. She had these huge portraits of dead relatives hanging everywhere. Give me a friendly-looking embalmed moose any day." He patted the snout of the nearest one.

"Photographs?" I asked.

"What?"

"The portraits," I said.

"Nah, they were paintings."

I stared at him. "You're kidding. Where are they now?"

"The art gallery," he said slowly, like it was suddenly sinking in that I might have wanted to see pictures of the people we came from. "I donated them before you and I moved out of here."

"Why? I never got to see them!"

"I know, I know," he said. "Bad call, maybe. But you were three. I had no idea you were going to be into art, and we needed room in the basement. I didn't want to sell them, in case you wanted to see them someday, and the art gallery jumped at the chance to take them. We can go look at them sometime, if you want."

Better than nothing. "What are they like?" I asked. "Do we look like anyone?"

"Oh, probably," he said. "I don't remember. They were all dark and atmospheric, and everyone looked depressed and desperate to get out of those stiff, stuffy clothes. Even our grandmother didn't want them, and she kept everything. She said she was sick of being stared at by dead people all the time. That's why they were in the basement, and if someone else wanted them, so much the better."

"Who painted them?"

He shrugged. "Can't remember. The same painter did all of them, though. I remember that much. Tell you what, I'll give the art gallery a call. We can visit. I donated some photos to the archives too. We can go see those as well, if you want."

I groaned. "Photos too, Zac? It's not like those take up tons of room."

Zac stared at me, a hurt look on his face, and I felt instantly like a spoiled brat. "Sorry, sorry. It's not like I expected you to carry them around the world with us. I'm a bit overwhelmed, that's all. It's weird being here. With all this. You grew up with everything. Our mother did too. I've never seen any of it before."

We'd spent almost my whole life traveling, without any links to any particular place. No parents. No grandparents. (None that talked to us, anyway.) We made friends everywhere we went, but Zac was really good at making money around the world — nannying, English tutoring for a rich family in Thailand, writing reviews or travel articles about obscure places — and we were always on the move. We hardly ever kept in touch after we left anywhere, and I could count on two fingers the people I'd known forever: Zac and Pierre, but like I said, we didn't see Pierre often. It had always been me and my brother against the world. Now here we were surrounded with this whole, long family history stretching back through time, and I felt totally disconnected from all of it, like I'd landed in a UFO.

We looked around us at the bazillion things we needed to sort in the next few months. Personally, I didn't see how we could possibly sell it all this summer in the slow, careful, top-dollar way that Zac wanted to do it, but there was no point telling him that. When Zac got something in his head, he stuck to it, no matter what.

"Overwhelmed," he echoed my thoughts. "You and me both."

I handed him a stack of papers. With the junk cleared off, the desk was that slick black I'd only seen happen with really old wood, like an altar in a Japanese temple. The top was smooth and shiny. Carvings of seaweed, shells, and sea creatures climbed the legs and drawers. "Have you seen this?"

"The desk? Yeah, our great-great-great —" He was counting off the greats on his fingers "— grandfather Clarence carved it."

"Seriously?" Mom had been an art historian, but I didn't know anyone in the family — apart from me — had ever *made* stuff. "When would that have been?"

"I don't know," Zac said. "Nineteen hundred, maybe? A bit after that? Mom had the desk upstairs for years, in the same room you're sleeping in now. I used to sneak in to touch the carvings when I was really little."

My mother's desk. I pictured the woman I only knew from photos, resting her elbows on it and staring out the window. Then I imagined my great-great-great-grandfather's hands carefully chiseling out each carving. This piece of furniture knew more about my family than I ever would.

"Can we keep it? I know we don't have room at home, but after we sell this house, we could afford a storage locker, right? To keep a few things until we're really, really sure we don't want them?"

I knew he'd like this idea about as much as he liked being called Dad-ee-o, but I didn't want to give up the only thing someone in our family had actually made with his own hands. If anything made me feel like I belonged in this family, it was this desk.

My brother tilted his head and looked at me, curious. "I can tell this means a lot to you. It could be a slippery slope, though. If we keep the desk, then what's to stop us from keeping a whole pile of stuff? I don't want to live my life with a storage locker full of things we haven't dealt with yet."

"I'm not asking for a locker full of stuff," I said. "I want this desk. You can do whatever you like with all the china, and the crystal, and the dog figurines, and the silver spoon collection, and —"

"Stop! Stop!" He covered his head with his hands.

"— and the Christmas ornaments, and the antique footstool, and the mangy moose heads, and —"

"Okay! Okay!" he said. "I won't sell the desk. We'll figure out how to store it so you can have it later. I'm sorry about the portraits at the art gallery."

"That's life," I said. "I can always take pictures of them when we visit and print them out, if I really want to."

"That would certainly be harder to do with a desk," he agreed, "although with 3D printer technology, maybe we could have it scanned, save the file, and *then* sell —"

I lobbed a cushion at him and hit the moose square in the antlers. My brother stood laughing underneath. "Kidding. *Kidding!* And watch it with those antlers."

"I know, I know. Vintage moose, right?"

Sigh. The summer stretched out ahead of me in an endless pile of boxes, towels, and knickknacks. At that point, I had no idea I was so close to something that would change everything.

Chapter Three

Outside, seagulls were calling like at home, but I didn't recognize the sloped ceiling above me, not right away. This happened a lot. So many times in my life, I'd spent the first moments of the morning trying to figure out where I was. In the past ten years, we'd lived in seven countries, some for a few months, and some for longer. I'd gotten used to Zac waking up one day with a sudden interest in teaching English in South Korea, or picking grapes in French vineyards. Two years ago, he decided we should have a home base, so we moved to a tiny island on the west coast of Canada, not far from Victoria. Zac got a few odd jobs, but I kept homeschooling so we could still take off every few months to explore a new country. The big difference was coming back to the same little house in the woods. This summer, we were supposed to be volunteering on a sheep farm in Iceland. Zac had already found a renter for our tiny house when we got the call from our grandmother's lawyer.

Now here I was, waking up in the attic room my mom once used as her office.

I propped myself on my elbows to look through the stained-glass window. It was a weird, square one that you could open at the top, but only enough to get your arm through. Ages and ages ago, servants lived up here, and this was probably one of the only windows. Zac said there wasn't even a fire escape back then, but before he was born, our mom turned this floor into a separate apartment, full of skylights and brightness. Zac grew up here, and so did I for the first three years of my life. Later, our grandmother rented it out. The tenants moved out a few weeks before we got here, leaving it empty and spotless, and we'd tried to keep it that way, except for the few things we'd brought with us (sleeping mats, sleeping bags, and clothes) or dragged up from downstairs (folding table, two lawn chairs, and some cooking things). When you spent all day, every day, sorting through piles of stuff in a dark, dusty room downstairs, this floor felt like a sparkling palace.

Through my door, I heard the clatter of dishes, Zac's I'm-trying-to-be-quiet voice, and then Pierre's.

"Morning," I called out.

"Morning, Sleepy Head," Zac called back. "We've got company, and he brought breakfast."

"*Bonjour!*" Pierre said. "Have you tried yet the *pain au chocolat* from the bakery on Fort Street?"

"Not yet, but give me a few seconds!" I shuffled out of my room, rubbing my eyes, and hugged each of them. "Hey, Pierre, how go the boat repairs?"

"Ah, I scraped the barnacles with a bit too much vigor, I'm afraid," he said. "I scraped so hard that I dinted the propeller, and so today I must order a new one. They are hard to get, though, and I feel like I may be here for a very long time."

"Sorry about the propeller," I said. "Hurray for you sticking around for a while. Especially if you bring *pain au chocolat.*"

He smiled. "How is it going for you here?"

"It's … uh … fascinating and overwhelming at the same time."

"Your grandmother, she had plenty of belongings."

"You got that right," I said. "I can't imagine what it was like *before* Zac cleared some of them out. He was telling me about a whole wall full of painted family portraits."

"Hey, I apologized for that already!" Zac placed two steaming mugs of milky tea on the folding table. "Grab the other mug please, Frida."

"Ah, the portraits." Pierre bit into a flaky *pain au chocolat.*

"You remember them?" I asked.

"I do indeed," he said. "I looked at them very closely the few times I visited your grandmother's apartment. They reminded me of a painting that I had for a time."

"A portrait?" I asked.

"Yes," he said. "Portraits are incredible, no? Each one says as much about the painter as it does about the subject, I think."

I nodded. "I saw a website once that showed paintings of the same thing by different artists. All the pictures were of, say, a bowl of fruit, but one artist used bright, surreal colors, and another was very realistic. Each painting had a completely different feeling. I can hardly wait to see those family portraits, to see our relatives but also to see what the artist thought of them."

"I'll call today to make an appointment," Zac said. "Pierre, these *pains au chocolat* are amazing!"

I mumbled agreement through a mouthful.

When we'd all finished the pastries and slurped up the last bit of tea, Zac dusted off his fingers. "Okay, now back to work. Did I tell you I found another three boxes of ancient dresses in the basement? I swear, we could open a costume museum with all the clothes and footwear in this place." He looked pained for a moment. "So, Pierre, are you *sure* you're not up for a morning of sorting through dusty boxes?

"Tempting, but I must decline," Pierre said. "I have an appointment with a propeller."

Zac turned to me. "*You're* joining me, though, right?"

"Yeah, sure," I said. "I just need to put on something other than pajamas."

Back in my room, though, instead of rummaging in my backpack for clothing, I flopped onto my sleeping mat. It had felt so weird to hear Pierre talking about our grandmother, someone I didn't even remember, here in this house where so many blood relatives had lived, long before I existed. Of course, back then, this had just been a cramped attic, but it still felt like it was swirling with people who came before me.

This was the smallest room in the whole house. Our great-great-great-grandfather's desk must have taken up most of the floor space when it was in here. Mom probably had it facing the window. I wondered what kinds of things she thought about when she gazed through this stained glass.

Wondering this felt strange and possibly like a really bad idea, like the first time I bit into raw octopus. For most of my life, my mother hadn't been a factor (never mind my mystery-father). She'd had Zac young with someone Zac had only met a few times. She had me seventeen years later, and she died in a car crash when I was one. It wasn't like I remembered her or knew what I was missing. That's what I'd always told myself. But here, in the house where I would have grown up, it was harder to believe.

If it hadn't been for the crash, this room would still be Mom's study. On this day in that alternate reality, maybe I'd have woken up in the bedroom next door. Zac would have been a way older brother that I hardly ever saw. Would he have a partner and kids by now — been a real Dad-ee-o? For sure, if he'd traveled the world, it would have been without me, and — *Stop*. I slammed my eyes shut. Why bother thinking about impossible things?

I rolled off my sleeping mat, grabbed an art history book, and read most of a chapter about art forgery before I was ready to get up. I threw on some clothes and hurried downstairs before my weird alternate-reality line of thought could catch up with me.

"Good morning," Hazeem said to a man who passed us on the sidewalk. He ignored us completely and kept walking. Hazeem looked at me and shrugged, and we crossed toward my grandmother's house.

"Who was that?" I asked.

"No idea," Hazeem said. "Just trying to keep things friendly."

"Good luck," I said. "People don't say hello much here. It's not like where Zac and I live. People are friendly there in general, but as soon as they saw us on our bicycles all the time — we don't have a car — it was like everyone on the whole island knew us. They'd cheer us on as we pedaled up hills, or they'd offer to bring our groceries home for us, so we wouldn't have to cart everything by bike."

"Sounds like home," Hazeem said. "Mom and I were talking about that, how people here pass each other on the sidewalk as if the other person didn't exist. We'd say hi, and they'd look at us all weird, so Mom and I decided to do something about it. We call it the Relentless Friendliness Project."

I laughed. "Seriously? That sounds like something Zac and I would do."

"You can join us, if you want," Hazeem said. "We say hi to people on the street. Some of them really get spooked, but others are so surprised that they say hi back. The older ones are better at it. Sometimes they'll even start a conversation. Mom and I swap stories at the end of the day. I'm way ahead so far."

"Way ahead?" By now, we were behind my grandmother's house, and I was wheeling an ancient three-speed up out of the basement. It was red with a white chain guard and cracked white tires. A bag of bike tools dangled from its handlebars. "How do you 'win' at Relentless Friendliness?"

"She's had conversations," he said. "But I actually made a friend and got a bike out of the deal too."

I froze. "So you only took me around to other book boxes as part of this competition with your mom?" Was there a reward for making friends with whoever looked the loneliest? Had he seen me from his apartment window, walking down to the book exchange box every single day before we met?

"No!" he said. "That's not what I meant! I would have *wanted* to get to know you when Pierre introduced us, but knowing that Mom and I had this project gave me extra courage."

I considered this for a moment. "You don't seem like someone who needs extra courage." He'd told me about missing his dead grandfather within about twenty-five seconds of meeting me, after all.

"Yeah, well, looks can be deceiving," he said. "You're seriously mad at me for wanting to get to know you? Or is it the bike? You don't have to —"

"No, it's —"

He looked so embarrassed and lonely and … unarmed …

Then I felt like a jerk for bugging him about this. "Sorry. It's been a weird few days."

He turned his head to one side and looked at me, like he was waiting for me to say more. I wasn't about to explain that I'd spent a chunk of the morning thinking about an alternate reality in which I actually had parents, or at least *a* parent. I'd never been able to weave my dead mother and non-existent father into casual conversation with someone I barely knew.

So I told him about the desk instead. "Zac wants to sell it, but I want to keep it. We don't have room to store it, though, and Zac doesn't want to pay for storage, so now he's trying to find someone to lease it to, as an art piece."

"Lease it?" Hazeem asked.

"Yeah, like renting," I said. "Someone would pay us for the privilege of having a hand-carved, antique desk in their house. Zac says the art gallery leases out art all the time."

"Sorry," Hazeem said, "but who is Zac?"

Damn. Apparently we were going to have this conversation anyway. "He's my brother and also my legal guardian. We're the last branch on the family tree. The end of the line." I locked my eyes on Hazeem's. This usually worked when I didn't want people to ask any questions.

"The desk sounds amazing," he said, his eyes still on mine. "I'd like to see it sometime."

"Sure." I leaned the bike away from me and looked at its flat tires and rusty chain. "Now, about this bike. It definitely needs some work, but I think it'll be okay. Let's bring it out to the sidewalk where there's better light."

We rolled the bike back around the front of the house and down to the grassy strip by the sidewalk. I put down the kickstand, pulled my pump from the bag of tools, and screwed off the valve cap of the front tire. I was pumping like crazy when I heard a low voice behind me. "Nice to see you again, Hazeem."

A man with a white beard and a red collared shirt stood at the front of a small group of adults. I sat crouched next to the road, sweating as I pumped up the tire, and they were looking around like they were in Disneyland. A few took pictures with their phones.

"Hi, John," Hazeem said. "This is Frida. She lives here." He pointed up the slope to my grandmother's house. "Frida, John is a tour guide … but I guess you figured that out already."

"Nice to meet you, Frida." John nodded and turned back to the group. "We'll stop here for a moment so I can tell you a little bit about this residence. It was built in 1911, after the Dunsmuirs sold off the land around the castle. This particular family had made its fortune as carpenters in the Klondike gold rush. Generally, it wasn't the people panning for gold who struck it rich, but rather those who provided services to them. Now we'll continue up this way." He nodded to us and led the group up the path toward the castle.

"This house is on a local tour?" I asked when they'd disappeared.

"Every week," Hazeem said. "My mother signed us up for one of the tours when we first got here, and when John found out we live on this street, he added a bunch of extra details about the families who used to live here. Now I see him all the time, and last week, he stopped to talk on the way back to his bicycle. Did you know your house is one of the only ones where the original family still lives there?"

Not for long, I thought and felt a pang as I imagined never again stepping into a room my mother had stepped into. (And what was up with that, anyway? A few weeks ago, I'd hardly ever thought about her, and now it was like she wouldn't leave me alone.)

I pushed that thought aside and smiled at Hazeem. "You're taking this Relentless Friendliness thing really seriously, making friends with everyone who walks past your house."

"It makes life more interesting." He looked around at the manicured lawns along the empty street.

"Are you glad you came here this summer?" I asked, but what I really wanted to know was if it helped. Did being in

Victoria stop him from thinking about that alternate reality where his grandfather was still alive and spending the summer with them in the Yukon? Because I thought being somewhere else could do that. I hadn't even thought about alternate realities (much) until we'd got here and were living in the same house that contained them all. Was this part of why Zac wanted to travel all the time, so all those alternate realities didn't gang up on him?

"I wouldn't want to be at home this summer without my grandfather," Hazeem said. "He would have wanted us to explore something new. Sometimes I imagine reporting to him everything I've seen and done in a day, especially about the people I meet. He could talk to anyone."

"So can you, I think."

"Thanks." He looked away, but not before I saw tears in his eyes.

"I wonder who we'll meet next," I said to change the topic.

He yawned and rubbed his face. "Who knows? Could be anyone."

Or almost anyone. Not the two people we most wanted to see — his grandfather, my mom. They were gone and never coming back.

Chapter Four

A loud *booooong* echoed through the house. At first, I thought my brother had changed his ringtone. Then I remembered our grandmother's doorbell.

"You'd think this was Buckingham Palace or something." Zac got up, slapped the dust off his shorts. I was wiping down the desk, surrounded by stacks of boxes three high. He looked at me. "Shall I get it then?"

"Yup. I'm not getting out of here any time soon," I said, "and if it's Hazeem, can you ask him in please? He wanted to see the desk."

"Will do." A few seconds later, I heard the front door click open, and a loud, cheery woman's voice asked after his personal relationship with Jesus Christ. I fully expected Zac to shut and lock the door before he could say *None of your business*, but he must have been desperate for fresh air and sunshine because he stepped out onto the porch and closed the door behind him. If I'd been able to get to the window, I'd have peeped through the curtains just to watch this conversation. No one could sell Zac anything he didn't want to buy, and I wouldn't have been surprised if he tried to sell her some of the women's clothing he'd found in the basement that morning.

I kept going with the desk. As my cloth glided over each surface, I imagined Clarence's fingertips running along one of the seashells, or servants' hands polishing the smooth top. Before we leased it to anyone, I was going to draw it, especially the carvings. They weren't perfect — the clams were lumpy-looking — but I loved them even more for *not* being perfect. They were real, hand-carved instead of mass-produced. This desk had personality.

I emptied the drawers, hoping for a trace of my mother — maybe an old piece of her stationery or a notebook — but all I got was a stack of tablecloths, a drawer full of napkin-holders, and a few extra sets of cutlery, in case of a sudden dinner party. I pulled out the top drawer as far as it would go and rubbed my cloth around the dark wood inside. I was digging my fingernail into the crevices around the edges when I spotted a tiny red ribbon, almost invisible against the wood. I picked at it and tugged. The entire drawer bottom shifted, and I froze. *Don't tell me I just busted the only thing in this whole house that I actually care about.*

Nothing looked broken, and the ribbon stayed stuck. I pulled on it again. With a crack and a scraping sound, a layer of wood came up. Underneath, a big, creamy canvas took up almost the whole base of the drawer. It looked old, stained with brown like someone had spilled tea on it a hundred years ago. I pinched an edge between my fingernails, eased it out, and flipped it over.

It was half as long as my arm, a painting of a woman who was about eighteen and looked part annoyed and part scared that I'd stuff her into the drawer again. She'd obviously been there for a while. Her clothing was dark and old-fashioned — I'd seen white, lacey collars like that in museums — and her hair was pulled back in a bun. Dangling earrings blended into the background, and the painting was so realistic that I almost expected her to raise a hand to her neck, cramped after all those years in the desk.

But what was she doing here? This wasn't like the random ten-dollar bills we'd found stuffed in nooks and crannies. This kind of hiding place took thought and tools and wood-working know-how. Also, our grandmother was into sets (dishes, porcelain raccoons, silver spoons, I could go on). So why would she let Zac get rid of all the paintings but one?

I bet someone else had put it here, a long time ago, and no one else ever knew. Maybe Great-great-great-grandfather

Clarence built this whole desk to hide the painting. Wait. If our grandmother hadn't known about the painting, then Zac probably didn't either. Otherwise, he would have mentioned the one in the desk drawer when I was disappointed about him donating the rest of them, right?

That meant this was one family heirloom that could be mine and mine alone.

The front door clicked open again, and I heard my brother's footsteps in the hall. "Sorry," I whispered to the woman in the portrait, slid her back into place, and slammed the drawer shut. I'd tell Zac eventually. But for now, I'd keep the portrait to myself. Just for a little while.

"You should try the bread," said Hazeem. "My mom made it. Traditional Yukon recipe." He handed me a thick slice.

We were standing on a lawn a few doors from the book exchange. About thirty or forty people were talking in clumps, plastic wine cups in hand. Two little kids raced between people's legs. Almost everyone else had gray hair.

"Nice crust," I said through a mouthful of bread.

"Sourdough, from a 120-year-old starter. The starter's the wild yeast and bacteria that make the bread rise."

I stopped chewing. "I'm eating 120-year-old wild yeast and bacteria?"

"Isn't it amazing? Mom got her starter from someone whose great-great-something-or-other came up from California in the Klondike gold rush —"

"Hey! *My* great-great-something-or-others were in that gold rush too. Isn't that what the tour guide said?" I popped another piece of bread into my mouth. No matter how gross the ancient yeast thing sounded, it tasted good.

"The gold rush dudes brought their starters from California so they could make bread whenever," Hazeem said. "In the winter they slept with the starters in their sleeping bags so the yeast didn't freeze, and they had to feed them flour every few days too."

"I'm eating something an ancient miner kept in his sleeping bag?" I peered at the bread. "This is getting weirder and weirder all the time."

Hazeem closed his eyes and smiled as he swallowed another mouthful of bread. "Think." His voice dropped as though he was suddenly narrating a documentary. "The bread you hold in your hand exists only because every generation fed the starter, kept it alive, and passed it to the next one. *You* are eating a living family heirloom, a piece of history." He ripped off another chunk of crust with his teeth and batted his eyelashes.

"The Yukon Tourism Board should definitely hire you," I teased, but I had to admit the whole sourdough thing was interesting. I loved that each generation knew the story of the starter, and 120 years of family members actively kept it from freezing or starving to death. Some of my ancestors couldn't be bothered to help keep small humans (like me) alive, never mind sourdough starters. Not that Zac and I were bitter about it, of course.

"Frida!" A hunched woman with a walker had toddled over to us, nodded at Hazeem, and smiled at me. "So nice to see you again."

"You … already know each other?" Hazeem asked.

"Uh —" This woman looked way older than anyone here (and believe me, *that* was saying something). I knew I'd have remembered meeting her —

She held out her hand. "I'm Anna Martin. I used to look after you when you were tiny. Your brother too. I was a friend of your grandmother's."

I shook her hand and said how pleased I was to meet her, like I knew I was supposed to, but really two thoughts were colliding in my head at once. *She knew my grandmother! Maybe she'll have stories to tell!* and *What if she's as weird as our grandmother was and this is going to be a really awkward conversation?* My eyes found Zac in the crowd, so I could bolt toward him if I needed to.

Anna was smiling at me, though. "Do you know that you're the spitting image of your —" She frowned and started counting on her fingers, as Zac had when he was talking about the desk. "What would it have been? Your great-great-grandmother. Yes, you look just like her. Her mother had Spanish blood and she had the most beautiful, thick, black hair, you know."

I touched my own short hair. I'd never thought about which relative it came from. The woman in the desk portrait had dark hair too, and maybe it was thick. That part of the painting was all shadows, so it was hard to tell. Could it have been my great-great-grandmother?

Nah. Why would her own father stuff her in a drawer instead of hanging her on the wall with everyone else?

"She was always so elegant," Anna said. "Of course, her hair was turning white when I knew her. The portrait in the hallway showed her as a young woman, though, and my, she was striking. She had a real flair for fashion too. Always very well dressed."

I looked down at my dirty cut-offs and baggy T-shirt. "*That* obviously skipped my generation."

Hazeem smirked, and Anna patted my arm. "I was never one for fashion, either. Your grandmother used to tease me about it when we were girls. There she was, styling herself after the women in the glossies, and I was wearing whatever clothes my mother gave me. We were an odd pair, that's certain."

I barely heard anything after *when we were girls*. That must have been like seventy-five years ago. For as far back as I could remember, Zac had been the only other leaf on our family tree that I'd let myself think about. Now here I was chatting about my grandmother's childhood with one of her playmates. I felt like one of those characters in an old-fashioned cartoon who gets hit in the head and his eyeballs zoom around and around.

Anna fiddled with something on her walker and turned it into a chair for herself. "Sorry, dears. These old legs aren't as strong as they used to be. I understand you've seen a bit of the world since last I saw you, Frida."

After weeks of trying to squeeze family stories out of doilies and teacups, here was a real, live person who'd lived across the street for almost a hundred years. I felt a surge of panic. Now that I'd found her, what if she keeled over before I could figure out what to ask first? "Did you ever see the desk my great-great-great-grandfather carved?" I blurted.

"Ah, yes," she said. "Your family was always very proud of it. Beautiful piece, that desk. I'm glad you still have it. I was worried when Zac donated those portraits. I was afraid he'd find another home for the desk too."

"Nope. We're keeping it," I said, "and we're going to the art gallery to see the portraits this week. Zac made an appointment, and I —"

I was about to tell her about the portrait I'd found in the desk when a man with a mustache placed a hand on Anna's shoulder. "Good to see you, old girl!"

She gave him a tight smile and turned back to me, but he started telling her about how he was going to repaint his house. "Wait 'til you see it! All the original colors!

Hazeem and I listened to him drone on for a while before we decided to play ring toss instead. We interrupted the monologue to say goodbye to Anna, and she squeezed my hand. "Welcome back. It's good to have you home."

That last word echoed in my head all through our game. *Was* this place home? Almost everyone connecting me to it was dead, and New York or Paris both felt more familiar. But Anna seemed to think I belonged here … because of a family history that I hardly knew anything about.

"Another game?" Hazeem asked.

He'd won by a landslide. Normally, I would've kept playing until I had at least evened out the score, but at that moment, I didn't have it in me. "I'm kind of beat, actually."

He laughed. "Literally. I beat you good."

"Har, har. Good game," I added, so he wouldn't think I was a sore loser. Looking around, I saw that Anna was gone. (*Shoot!* I'd been hoping to talk to her again. I wanted to ask her more about my grandmother and tell her about the portrait in the desk.) It looked like my brother had taken off too. "I think I'll head home,"

I asked around and found out Zac had gone back to the house. I said goodnight to Hazeem and left.

The front door was wide open, and Zac was talking inside.

Chapter Five

"Hullo?" I called in.

"Frida!" my brother called back. "Great news! You've met Liz, right?"

Liz? Auctioneer Liz? *I-wouldn't-let-her-anywhere-near-our-grandmother's-stuff-because-auction-houses-take-a-huge-cut* Liz?

Yup. She was standing next to the desk, one hand resting on its shiny surface. "Lovely to see you again! Your brother has been telling me the history of this beauty! Hand-carved right here, in this very house!" She spoke with so many exclamation marks that I shot a nervous look at my brother.

He stood a few feet away from her, arms crossed over chest, a smug look on his face. Whatever the smugness was about, though, he looked perfectly calm — not at all like they'd just found a portrait hidden in a drawer. That would have definitely come up by now, right? Like the instant I stepped into the house?

"You remember that Liz works at an auction house," Zac said.

"Yes," I said slowly.

"I mentioned our situation," Zac said, "and the idea of leasing out this desk. She offered to help identify the wood ..."

Probably just to get her foot in the door, I thought. Now she'd keep bugging us the way she was bugging Anna, eager to sell anything she could get her hands on. I should have given my brother a stronger warning about that.

"... ebony, so it could command a high price ...," Liz was saying.

"If we were selling," Zac said, "which we're not."

I smiled. Zac didn't need warning. Liz had met more than her match. She just didn't know it yet.

"A real loss for the market," she said. "I'm sure educated collectors would jump at a chance to have this piece. In fact, *I* would jump at a chance to have this piece in my living room. Even if I was only leasing for a few years."

I felt my stomach twist. Why had I agreed when Zac suggested renting out the desk? Why wasn't I more specific about who to lease it to? What was it about Liz that bothered me so much, anyway? That she'd called me Frances?

That she seemed obsessed with selling stuff? That her eyes seemed hard, even when she smiled? All of the above?

"Is that an offer?" Zac asked.

"Absolutely! This piece will be a perfect match for …"

She droned on, but I'd stopped listening. The painting was still in the desk. What if she —?

Calm down, I told myself. Her house was completely gutted at the moment, and no way would this desk fit into the tiny cottage where she was living now. What did I think she was going to do, go back to the barbecue and find twenty of the most able-bodied seniors to help her drag it back to her lair?

"You won't be able to take the desk for a while," I said. "Trouble is, we need someone to take it off our hands as soon as possible."

Zac raised an eyebrow at me. I nodded and smiled big, praying that he'd play along.

"Yes," he said quickly. "As you can see, it's a big piece, and we'll need to have it relocated as soon as possible to finish off our work here."

She gazed at him and sighed. Then she turned and winked at me. (Yuck.) "Your dad drives a hard bargain."

I looked at Zac and smothered a smirk. He was rolling his eyes, but Liz didn't seem to notice. "I'll try to get it out of your hair as soon as possible," she said. "Luckily, in my business, I know people with big trucks. I could have it out as soon as tomorrow."

She looked back and forth between us, and while her eyes were on me, Zac caught my eye and shook his head ever so slightly. That's how I knew not to panic when he said, "Now you're talking. I'll draw up a leasing contract and get back to you as soon as I can. This really is a brilliant stroke of luck, and now I think we've taken up quite enough of Liz's time, haven't we, Frida? Thanks again for your help with the wood ID."

"A pleasure, Zac." She gave him her hand to shake. "Nice to see you again, Phoebe."

My brother and I managed to keep straight faces until we closed the door behind her and saw her reach the sidewalk.

"Phoebe?" Zac asked, laughing.

"She called me Frances the first time we met," I said, "and you should hear all the variations Hazeem got. She remembered your name perfectly, though."

"Because I'm the one who's going to sign the contract," he said. "Supposedly."

"The imaginary contract, right?" I asked. "You're not seriously thinking of leasing the desk to her, right?"

"Why not?" he asked, but I could tell he was teasing.

"You saw how she was drooling over it. I'm sure she'll take good care of it. She seems like someone who cares a lot about appearances."

"Blech," I said. "I don't want our great-great-great-grand-father's work hanging out at her house for the next decade. All she cares about is making money and showing off."

Zac smirked and looked around the living room at the crystal, the moose heads, and the fancy high ceilings. "She would have fit right in with this family. She and old Clarence might have had a lot in common, in fact."

I sighed.

"Don't worry," he said. "It'll take me a while to sort out what a leasing contract should look like. I'll work at finding a better offer in the meantime, and then we can turn her down. I didn't like her much either."

Later that evening, when my brother-dad was brushing his teeth, I snuck back down, pulled the portrait from its hiding place, and brought it up to my room. It was too big to hide in my sketchbook, but it fit into the oversized book on conceptual art that Hazeem had found at the book exchange. Zac would never find it in there. Not only because he would never open a book on conceptual art unless I forced him to, but also because he was super particular about privacy, both mine and his. He wouldn't set foot in my room without asking first, and even though that was a great thing, it made me feel bad too, because now I was actually using it to hide something from him.

It wasn't like I was going to hide it forever, though — only until I could figure out who the woman in the painting was and why our great-great-great-grandfather had hidden her away. Luckily, I now knew one living person who might be able to solve the mystery.

Chapter Six

The house was silent when I woke up. I rolled over in my sleeping bag, remembered the painting and Anna, and sprang out of bed. If Zac asked, I'd tell him I was going out for a few hours to sketch and read. I might knock on Anna's door to show her some of my drawings. My brother had no reason to think I was doing anything unusual, I told myself. *Just relax.*

And I did, when I saw Zac's note on the counter — *Gone to get groceries.*

Perfect. I ate a banana in three bites, downed a glass of apple juice, grabbed my sketchbook and the conceptual art book, and hurried down the stairs.

"Good morning!" Hazeem waved from a window across the street. He lived in an upstairs apartment of the house, and I knew Anna lived on the main floor (possibly in the apartment where the curtain was now opening a crack and closing again).

"Are you running surveillance over there, or what?" I asked.

"Nope. Cleaning windows. Unfortunately." He waggled the rag and spray bottle back and forth. "I was shaking a bottle of orange juice this morning, and I may have forgotten to check if the lid was on."

"Oops." I crossed the street and was on the front porch, trying to figure out which of the six little buzzers to press when the front door flew open.

"Come in, come in!" Anna beamed at me, looking especially tiny in the enormous doorway. Behind her, Hazeem rushed down a tall staircase that twirled in on itself like a snail's shell. There was a moment of confusion while each of them tried to figure out who I was visiting.

"Both of you," I lied, not wanting to hurt Hazeem's feelings.

"Do come in." Anna stood back to let us into her apartment. "Welcome, welcome. Have a seat."

This place was nothing like my grandmother's. It was bright and smelled of lemony floor polish. Also, I couldn't see an antique anywhere. She had a futon with an orange-and-brown afghan folded neatly at one end. The coffee table was light-colored wood, and one thin newspaper lay folded in the middle of it. Very full but tidy bookshelves covered the walls. After weeks at my grandmother's house, this place was like breathing fresh air again.

"Will you have some tea?" Anna asked.

"Oh. No, thank you. I'm not a big tea drinker, and I just had breakfast. I brought something to show you, though." I set my books on the table, pulled out the painting, and explained about finding it in the desk. "I thought the woman might be the great-great-grandmother you mentioned last night."

Anna took the canvas from me and pressed her lips together. "Only with a lot of imagination. The hair is the same, but your great-great-grandmother was bigger-boned. With smaller eyes and a different nose. Her skin was more olive-colored too."

"Do you recognize her at all?" Hazeem asked. I'd filled him in on certain family details during our ring toss game, mainly the fact that I didn't know any.

Anna shook her head and laid the portrait on the coffee table. "She doesn't look familiar."

"Oh." I let out my breath all at once. If Anna didn't recognize her, no one else would.

For a few seconds, the three of us stared at the painting. I imagined my great-great-great-grandfather's hands placing it in the drawer and pressing the false bottom over top of it.

Maybe, whoever she was, she died an early death, and he never got over it. Maybe it was his sister — although a sister would probably get a place on the wall, come to think of it.

So maybe it was a girlfriend whose portrait he'd kept all through getting to know my great-great-great-grandmother, but when they married, Great-great-great-grandma put her foot down. No portraits of ex-girlfriends on the walls of *her* house. He built the desk, carving sea creatures to distract anyone who might be poking around at the bottoms of drawers, and all those months of carving were like spending time with his lost …

"Hmm."

I looked up from the portrait to see both Hazeem and Anna watching me. The eye-rollingly sappy story I'd invented popped like a soap bubble, and I felt my face go red.

"I don't think she was from here," Anna said. "The clothes don't look right. No one in your family would have used earrings for a portrait either, Frida. Your great-grandmother nearly fainted when your grandmother came home with her ears pierced. It was a family scandal. The painting style is different too, and I'm no expert, but I don't think this one was done by Sophie Pemberton like all the others."

"You know the name of the painter?" I asked. "Zac couldn't remember."

Hazeem reached over, picked up the painting, and squinted at it.

"Oh, yes," Anna said. "Sophie Pemberton was a marvel. She was very famous here from 1900 to about 1910. She did portraits for many well-to-do people in Victoria. I found that out later, but as a child, I used to stand in Gloria's hall-way staring at the paintings. They made me feel like I had met those people, even the ones who had died before I was born."

"It looks like there was a label on the back at some point." Hazeem held up the portrait and pointed to a discolored rectangle on the back. Then he peered at the painting again. "There! Bottom right corner! It's smudged, but it's a signa-ture. I think it says *J. Nille*. We could look that up online … I mean, *you* could. Mom's on a big anti-technology kick right now. She promised me two hundred bucks if I stay offline this summer. Mostly offline, anyway. I'm allowed to use the computers at the library, but there's always a wait, and they time out after half an hour."

"So *that's* why you know so much about book boxes and what's going on in the neighborhood," I said. "Don't let your mom talk to Zac or they'll start a club. He's been on an anti-technology kick my whole life — when it comes to me, anyway."

"Wise guardians," said Anna.

Hazeem rolled his eyes. "You'd join their club, wouldn't you?"

"Absolutely."

"*Anyway,*" I said, "I could look up J. Nille on Zac's phone, but I still won't know who the woman in the portrait is, or why it was hidden ... or why my family was so into portraits anyway. There were photographers back then — I'm reading a book about a local one right now — so why sit around getting a portrait painted?"

"That last question I can answer," Anna said. "Only the very rich could afford to get a painting done."

"Oh," I said. "You mean they did it to show off?"

"To ... establish their place in society, perhaps," said Anna. "People who were born into money looked down at anyone who'd worked for it. Some wealthy families spent their whole lives trying to prove that they were as sophisticated as the upper class. Gloria — your grandmother — found this focus on status terribly dull. It's part of why she left."

"To Regina," I told Hazeem. "That's where my mother was born."

"Eventually, yes," said Anna. "But Gloria moved to Hollywood first."

"*Hollywood?*"

"I don't remember what gave her the idea," Anna said. "She was only seventeen. She talked about it for weeks beforehand, but I thought she was making up stories until one morning she was gone. She sent a few postcards — never with a return address — and then, years later, she showed up on our doorstep looking like ... well ... like life had been difficult. She took off again soon afterward, and next I heard from her, she was in Regina and pregnant with Kimmy."

I turned to Hazeem. "My mother."

"I figured," Hazeem said. "Hey, wait a minute! Maybe Frida's grandfather was some famous ancient movie star!"

"Pshaw!" Anna said. "People who were young in the fifties are *not* ancient."

Hazeem reddened, but Anna was laughing. "She wasn't pregnant yet, anyway. That happened a few years later. Frida's grandfather was a hamburger cook at the drive-in where Gloria was a server."

"Hollywood sounded more glamorous," I said. Not that I was hoping for glamour, of course. I'd have settled for finding out about the woman hidden in the desk. I slid the painting back into the book. "Well, thanks, Anna. I should probably get going now."

"Thank you for coming, dear."

Hazeem looked back and forth between us like we'd both lost our minds. "Hold on. What happens next?"

"What do you mean?" I asked.

"What's the next step in solving the mystery?"

"I don't know," I said. "I'll look up J. Nille online, but no search engine's going to tell me what I really want to know. And if he was a local artist who died a hundred years before the Internet was invented, I might not find out anything at all."

"Forget the computer," Anna said. "Didn't you say you'll be seeing your family's collection at the art gallery? Why not bring this portrait along and ask if they know anything about the artist?"

"I can't." The words were out of my mouth before I thought of what to say next. "It's … uh … if I bring this one along, the gallery might want us to donate it too, and … uh …" Wow, I was a terrible liar. I took a deep breath and let it out slowly. "Okay. Here's the thing. Before I can pull out this portrait at the art gallery, I have to tell Zac that it exists."

"Ah," Anna said. "That *is* an important consideration. Are you afraid he'll want to donate it as well, or sell it?"

I shook my head. "He still feels bad about donating the other portraits. I'm sure he'd let me keep this one. Without a frame, it doesn't take up much space."

"So …" Hazeem stared at me like I was a crazy-hard math problem.

I looked down at my hands. "Zac remembers most of the stuff in the house from when he was growing up. He remembers our mom and our grandmother. He even knew his dad."

Super awkward silence. Except for the voice in my head — *What are you doing? You never talk about this stuff to … well, to anyone. Not even Zac. Why the sudden gush?* Maybe it was the soft way Anna was looking at me, or maybe it was because she'd known me as a baby, and she'd known my mom, and our grandmother, and our great-grandparents too.

"You want to own it for a bit before you share it," she said. "You want to know one thing about your family that hasn't been passed down from your brother."

"Exactly," I said, "not that I —"

"It's fine, dear," said Anna. "I grew up as one of nine. Almost everything I owned was a hand-me-down, and the first time I got a brand-new, store-bought dress, I spent the longest time looking at it and savoring it before I tried it on. Zac is a perceptive young man. He'll understand if you wait a few days to tell him about the painting."

I nodded. None of us said anything.

"You know," said Hazeem, "you don't have to bring the portrait to the gallery. You could just ask about J. Nille while you're there. Say you saw one of his paintings at a friend's house. You're at a friend's house now, right, looking at the painting? So you won't be lying."

Anna frowned. "Is your grasp of the truth always this slippery, young man?"

"A sleuth's gotta do what a sleuth's gotta do," Hazeem said, "and if Frida's telling Zac about the painting in a few days anyway, what difference does it make?"

"Now that you mention it," I said, "I bet he'll love that the painting comes with a story, first finding it in the desk and then trying to figure out who painted it. *Value added,* he'll call it."

"It *is* value added," said Anna. "I'm enjoying this whole adventure thoroughly, myself."

"So you'll ask about J. Nille at the gallery?" Hazeem asked.

"Sure," I said. After all, what did I have to lose?

Chapter Seven

"Zac!" I stomped over to the kitchen — and only got about three feet in that direction before an ugly red-and-green tablecloth fell off a stack of boxes onto my head. "Agh! This place is driving me crazy!"

"What's all the yelling about?" Zac poked his head out of the kitchen doorway, and I tossed the tablecloth at him, narrowly missing one moose. My brother looked at me, perplexed, shook out the tablecloth, folded it neatly and placed it on a box next to him. "What's gotten into you?"

"The desk!" I said. "I *told* you I was drawing these things on the desk. I asked you not to move them because I wasn't done yet. You've got a whole house to organize, and you have to mess with the spoons anyway? How would *you* feel if I started messing with your pricing system?"

He looked at me blankly.

I waved my hand at the desk where I'd arranged three teacups and a pile of thirty-seven silver teaspoons. "Don't pretend you don't know what I'm talking about, Zac. I have documentary evidence." I flipped through my sketchbook, found the page where I'd outlined the position of everything — right before asking him not to touch anything so I could finish the drawing later — and I held it up. "This teacup was over there, and there were more spoons before. There was a candlestick holder too. I didn't put it in the drawing, but it's gone now."

"Frida," he said, "you know I wouldn't do that."

I froze. That was true. "Then … someone's been in here."

"Whoa," he said. "Let's not jump to conclusions." But the slight lift of his left eyebrow suggested that he was jumping to conclusions himself. He had an incredible poker face that worked perfectly when he was haggling with marketplace vendors in Istanbul or staring down security guards at the Vatican who wanted me to wear longer shorts, but I could always see when he was bluffing. "Maybe Pierre popped by while we were out," he suggested. "It's the most logical explanation. Why don't I text him to ask?" He patted down all his pockets and, for once, found his phone in one of them.

"You think he popped by to poke around, and he pocketed a handful of silver spoons and stole a candlestick holder while he was here?"

Zac shook his head like he was trying to shake out an idea. "I'll just text to see if he knows anything." Sure, he was sounding all responsible-adulty, but I could imagine his text to Pierre: *Help! There's been a break-in!*

"I bet it was Liz," I said, stating the obvious.

"Why would an antique dealer risk a criminal record for spoons and a candlestick holder?" Zac countered.

She was looking for the painting, I thought ... except, of course, that was ridiculous. Just because *I* was obsessed with a random portrait didn't mean that the creepy auction-house person from down the street wanted it. Besides, how would she even know it existed? Zac had been with her the whole time she was here, and *he* didn't know about the painting, so it's not like he would have pulled open the desk drawer, lifted the false bottom, and showed it to her.

"Was there anything she was interested in, apart from the desk?" I asked.

"A few items," he said. "The poker thingies for the fireplace, a few of the classic books on the shelves, and the wall clock in the kitchen. She saw it through the doorway and announced that it's a mid-century atomic starburst clock in excellent condition. I think she expected me to be impressed, but I *knew* that already."

I looked around. Poker thingies? Check. Still present and accounted for. Mid-century atomic starburst clock? Check. No gaps in the bookshelves either, and nothing else seemed to be missing.

Zac's phone buzzed. "You were right, Frida. Pierre wasn't here. It looks like someone *did* come in while we were gone." He picked his way between the boxes and examined the pile of spoons. "That candlestick holder was from the 1800s, not much to look at, but someone who knew their stuff would have recognized that it was worth taking. Also, it looks like she took the seven rarest silver spoons in this whole pile, not just the ones on the top."

"Are you calling the police?" I asked. "Will you tell them it was Liz?"

He pressed his lips together. "I want to, but I don't, you know? I think it probably *was* her, but it's not like we have any solid evidence."

I held up my sketchbook.

"I know, I know," he said. "But I mean, we can't go accusing a neighbor based on suspicions. And imagine what the police would say about this place. We lock the doors, but the windows don't even close fully. Everything's all over the place. We're going to look way more suspicious than the rich antique-tycoon from down the street."

He had a point.

"I'll look into getting those windows fixed ASAP though," he said. "And believe me, I'm going to have a word with Liz."

"Do you think she's dangerous?" I asked. "Will she break in again?"

He shook his head and smiled. His eyebrows were relaxed this time, though, and I felt like we were on solid, confident Zac-ground again. "I'll have a word with her," he said, "and I'm sure that after that, she'll steer clear of us. She cares a lot about her reputation, and *cat burglar* wouldn't look good on her resumé."

I shrugged. "Okay. I trust you."

"Can I have that in writing?" he teased.

"Watch it, Dad-ee-o."

"You're not going to believe this," I told Hazeem as I closed the door of the house behind me. I had a rear rack for a bicycle in one hand. The old bicycle I'd found down in the basement was waiting for us at his place. "Someone broke in to our place the other day."

"What?" He looked around like the burglar might still be hiding behind the hydrangea bushes. "How?"

I told him about the faulty windows. "Our friend Pierre came and sealed them shut on the ground floor." All but one, which he had to order a spare part for, I thought, but I wasn't going to say that out loud as I crossed the street. "The person stole a candlestick holder and some rare silver spoons."

"Random," said Hazeem.

"Not really," I said. "Zac says that someone who knew about antiques would have recognized them as worth stealing."

"You mean ..." His eyes opened wide, and he tilted his head in the direction of Liz's house.

I shrugged. "That's what we're thinking."

"But why would she do that?" he asked. "Why not ask to buy them?"

"Maybe she has to pay for all the renos?" I joke when I'm mega-uncomfortable.

"Did you call the police?"

"Zac didn't want to," I said. "He went to talk to her instead."

"And?"

"He told her someone had been in the house while we were out," I said. "He looked her right in the eyes then, in his best fake-out stare. She didn't miss a beat, just got all sympathetic and put her hand on his arm and said how sorry she was. He added that the windows were sealed shut now, and she flinched, but then she asked whether he'd thought of a price for leasing the desk, and when he told her how much he was asking, she laughed and said he clearly needed professional help to assess his inheritance. He told her to back off or else, and he left."

"Wow," Hazeem said. "Who knew this sleepy neighborhood would have so much drama?"

I rolled my eyes. "Tell me about it. I'm glad the windows are sealed, but what do I say to her if I see her in the street?"

"Wow," he said again as we went around the back of his house to the locked-up bicycle. The day before, I'd inflated the tires, greased the chain, wiped everything down, and adjusted the brakes. It was a good-looking bike. Retro and quirky. Hazeem was thrilled.

"Once we get this rack on the bike," I told him, "you can strap on a box of books, no problem. You'll barely notice the weight."

We crouched by the old three-speed in the shade beside his house, close enough to the sidewalk to be Relentlessly Friendly, but far enough from the pavement so we didn't fry in the heat. Inside, a doorbell sounded, and through Anna's open window, I heard her get up, shuffle across the living room, and open her apartment door.

"How do you know so much about bikes anyway?" asked Hazeem.

"Zac's fault," I said. "He says the less we spend on transportation, the more money we have left over for travel. That's why we own bikes instead of a car."

A familiar woman's laugh floated out through Anna's window. "No, no, dear. I *know* you don't have anything for the auction house, but I wonder if you could help me with a local history project. Zac tells me his family has lived in that house for over a hundred years?"

Hazeem and I looked at each other. Liz obviously wasn't giving up.

"That's right," Anna was saying. "I was friends with his grandmother when we were schoolgirls."

"I'm sorry for your loss then," said Liz, "and I imagine you'll be eager to help your friend's grandchildren. You see, Zac plans to sell everything, but he's determined to do it himself. I've explained that, with my connections, he could reach buyers with a true appreciation for local history and earn far more than he ever could online. But he won't listen, so I'm appealing to you, as a family friend, to help him see some sense. Grief can certainly cloud our thinking, and I'd hate to see him regret this later."

I clapped a hand over my mouth. She was painting herself as Saint Liz, our family's new guardian angel! Hazeem raised an eyebrow at me. I shook my head and put my finger to my lips.

"Now, Liz," said Anna, "I'm sure Zac's late grandmother would be pleased about your concern for his welfare, but the fact remains that he is a fully-grown man quite capable of making his own decisions. I've been alive too long to think it's any of my business what another adult does with his family's belongings."

"Well!" Liz sounded like she'd been slapped. "It depends whether you see the objects as personal belongings or cultural heritage."

"If you're concerned about cultural heritage," Anna said, "you'd best convince Zac to donate everything to the Royal B.C. Museum, where it can be enjoyed by all, not just by a private buyer."

I let out a snort and buried my face in my arm. Liz said something so quiet that I couldn't make it out. A few seconds later, we heard doors close, and footsteps hurried along the sidewalk. Hazeem and I stayed right where we were. Relentless Friendliness was on permanent hold where Liz was concerned.

Chapter Eight

Zac and I had been going to art galleries for as long as I could remember. When I was really little, we'd play games like I spy, or he'd carry me around and I'd point to whatever I wanted to see. Eventually, I started bringing my sketchbook. I'd copy paintings I liked, or at least try to copy the colors with my colored pencils.

There are art galleries, and there are *Art Galleries*. I mean, if someone told me to draw a random European one, I'd make it a huge, white stone building with pillars and a ginormous front door, narrow at the bottom and wide at the top, so it looked like it was towering over you, shouting "Heed me! I will impress you!" The Victoria Art Gallery wasn't at all like that. It had more of a "Psst, here I am" vibe — a low building on a side street, tucked behind tall trees and a little parking lot. Two sculptures — wooden and metal shapes — stood out front, like the place needed something quirky so you could tell there was art inside.

"So," Zac said, "ready to meet the fam?"

"Good question." Usually, when I stepped into a gallery, I was thinking of the future. *Would my work be here someday?* Now I was coming in to see people from our family's past. It was like coming to collect bits of myself that I hadn't known I'd lost, and it was more than a little weird.

"Welcome!" A woman by the front desk stepped forward with a big smile. She was about Zac's age and looked exactly like someone working in an art gallery *should* look, bright and colorful, with a star-shaped nose piercing and turquoise cat's-eye glasses. "I'm Jennifer. Nice to meet you both. Is this your first visit?"

I nodded. "We've been to plenty of other art galleries, though. We always go when we travel."

"Zac was telling me," said Jennifer. "He also told me you're a gifted artist."

I shot my brother a look. Who phones up an art gallery and winds up bragging about his little sister? Next thing, he'd have me haul out my sketchbook to show her what I'd been drawing lately — the house, the bicycle we'd lent to Hazeem, the carvings on the desk, yesterday's teacup — like Jennifer might squeal and rush to hang them in the gallery between Emily Carr and Lawren Harris.

"Sorry," she said. "I made that awkward, didn't I? I meant that I know you have a special interest in these paintings. I'm excited to show them to you. We only have room to display a small part of our collection. I don't often get to show visitors the vault, and that's where your family's portraits are. Follow me." She led us down the hall.

"Psst," I whispered to Zac. "Our family's in a vault. Like a national treasure."

"The great-great-greats would be so pleased," he whispered back.

We reached a locked metal door with key-card entry. Jennifer swiped us through. Stairs. More locked doors. More stairs. More doors.

"Sophie Pemberton," Jennifer said. "She was the artist who did your family's portraits. Born here, studied painting in Europe, and won international awards before coming back to do portraits for the city's richest families … Then she got married and gave up painting altogether."

"What!?" I asked. "Why?"

"Many reasons," Jennifer said. "She was in a bad horse accident. She married a man who already had a bunch of kids, and she would have been expected to look after them. Also, many people — including her husband, I imagine — believed that respectable ladies didn't work. Men were supposed to look after anything that had to do with money, so if a woman was earning it, people thought her husband couldn't look after her properly."

"Glad I live in *this* century," I said.

"You and me both." Jennifer swiped her security card yet again and let us into the vaults. The walls were whitewashed, and the air was cold. "I should have told you to bring sweaters. We keep the temperature low to preserve the artwork."

She led us through rooms full of shelves and cabinets. It was all storage, no art hanging on the walls anywhere. We stopped next to a rack of paintings. Jennifer pulled a pair of gloves from a pocket and reached for a very small canvas with swishes of pastel colors. "Check this out. It's a Matisse."

Zac and I stared at it. "A Matisse? Here in Victoria?" It seemed about as unlikely as a Drake concert at the North Pole.

"When Frida was six," Zac told Jennifer, "we were in Copenhagen and saw Matisse's *The Green Stripe*. You know the portrait where the shadows are all green?"

Jennifer nodded. "I've never seen it myself, but yes, I know the one you mean."

"Well, Frida thought it was hilarious that a painter could get the skin color all wrong and still get into a world-famous art gallery. She drew everyone with green faces for a while, and every new city we went to, we checked for Matisse paintings. Just for fun. I had no idea there was one a few blocks from where I grew up."

"You've followed Matisse all over the world?" Jennifer looked at my brother like he was too good to be true.

I turned away to hide my smirk. Zac swore up and down that he wasn't an art nerd — that art was *my* thing, not his — but these two were totally geeking out over this.

"We travel a lot," Zac said, looking all modest. "Looking for Matisses became one of our things. How did this one get here, anyway?"

Jennifer was still looking starry-eyed. "People leave us artwork in their wills. That's probably the story here."

They smiled at each other, and I was starting to feel like a third wheel, but luckily, they snapped out of it, and Jennifer pulled out a rack of paintings near the bottom. "Speaking of donations, these are your family's Sophie Pemberton portraits."

She lifted out one, brought it to the nearest table, and lifted out another, until we were staring down at four long-dead family members. Zac was right — the paintings were dark and heavy-looking, kind of how our grandmother's living room felt with the curtains closed. They still blew me away, though. Like Anna said, looking at one made you feel like you were meeting the person. Trouble was, I wasn't sure I *wanted* to meet people like these. Every single one looked snooty and unhappy. At least the woman in my hidden portrait seemed to know how to smile.

"That was our great-great-great-grandfather, Clarence." Zac pointed to an older man with a white handlebar moustache and a coat that looked too tight for his belly. He was nothing like the kind, thoughtful guy I had imagined creating those sea creatures, or the gentle romantic thinking back to his long-lost girlfriend. He looked more like he'd spent his life peering down his nose at everyone.

"I thought he'd be more cheery looking," I said.

Zac shrugged and turned to Jennifer. "We have a desk that he built."

"It's gorgeous," I said. "Dark wood with all these sea creatures and seashells carved on the drawers and legs."

"We're trying to lease it out," said Zac, "until Frida is old enough to have a place of her own. It's up for grabs, if you're in the market for huge, beautiful furniture." He waggled his eyebrows at her. I groaned. She laughed, and we turned back to the paintings. Zac pointed at Clarence and pulled a long, serious face that suddenly made them look a lot alike.

"That," I said, "is very scary."

Jennifer put back some of the portraits and brought out more. Most of them were about half as tall as me — big enough to make me wonder how they all fit on the walls. Did our ancestors cover every available space with paintings? Or did they alternate them, depending on the season or the visitor? Maybe someone had made fun of their smaller J. Nille painting at some point, so they decided to go big or go home?

Jennifer laid the seventh painting on the table, and my hand flew to my mouth. "It's me! It's me with a silly hat and a neck tie."

The girl in the painting was younger than I was, with long braids, and she was sitting on a high-backed chair with a book in her lap, looking right at us. We had the same dark hair, rounded nose, and big eyes. It had to be my great-great-grandmother, my "spitting image," as Anna said.

"Wow," said Zac. "I grew up seeing that painting, and I never clued in until now. Crazy, right? How many people know they could have passed for their great-great-grand-mother's twin?"

It was a little creepy — as if DNA from a bunch of gener-ations between us had been completely erased — but it was exciting too, like I'd suddenly found out I was part of a secret club. Did she and I have other things in common, apart from our looks? Like maybe she could flare her nostrils really quickly like I could (and Zac couldn't)? Or she preferred strawberry ice cream over chocolate?

"Would you like a picture of yourself with this painting?" Jennifer fished out her phone and asked Zac for his number. Right after she pressed send, her phone pinged, and she frowned. "Darn. I have another meeting soon. I completely lost track of time."

On the way out of the vault, she asked us questions about other galleries we'd visited and our favorite artists. "This has been such a pleasure," she said when we reached the front door again. Even though Zac already had her cell number, she handed me her card, like I was some important art professional. "In case you have any more questions."

This was my opening. I focused on Jennifer's face, not looking at Zac. "Do you happen to know anything about a local artist called J. Nille? I was looking at a painting at a friend's house a while ago. It was an old one, and that was the name in the corner. I looked up *J. Nille painter* online but couldn't find anything."

"The name doesn't ring a bell," said Jennifer. "Maybe it was an amateur artist?"

I doubted it. There was no way that painting was done by an amateur. Unless, of course, J. Nille was a woman whose husband didn't want anyone to know she could paint, in case they offered her money for her work. "I guess so," I said. "I'll let my friend know. Thanks."

I stole a glance at my brother to see if he'd noticed anything strange about my J. Nille questions. If he did, I couldn't tell. He and Jennifer were beaming at each other as if I wasn't there at all.

Chapter Nine

"*The Great Mystery of the Relative in the Desk Drawer* is a total bust," I told Hazeem that evening. We were sitting on his front porch, eating thick slices of sourdough bread with butter. "Zac and I are going to the provincial archives tomorrow to look at some family photos, which might be helpful, but I'm not getting my hopes up. Looks like I'll have to give him the painting straight up, no value added."

"No value added except that you think Liz might have been trying to steal it," Hazeem said.

I smiled. "Yeah, but when I think about it, that really makes no sense. There's no way for her to know it exists, and what would she want with an old family portrait by a nobody painter anyway?"

"Maybe when you tell Zac you found the painting, he'll have insider information," Hazeem said.

I shrugged and stuffed the last bite of bread into my mouth.

"Can I come to the archives with you?" he asked.

"Mawagfft," I said.

"Was that *be my guest*?"

I nodded and swallowed. "It'll be easier to recognize her if we have two sets of eyes on the job."

"We'll examine the painting and memorize every detail," Hazeem said, "like in the movies where they have to study a set of instructions and then eat them to destroy the evidence."

"If you eat that painting, I'll never forgive you."

"Okay, okay. I won't eat the painting."

"Thank you."

"No problem. That's what friends are for."

"Wow." Zac peered at a dog-eared photo in a thin file folder. Hazeem and I sat on either side of him. Most of the other long tables at the archives were empty. "The house looked a lot better then than it does now. No paint flaking off. The steps weren't sagging yet."

"Do you think the windows closed properly back then?" I joked.

"Probably not," Hazeem said. "Maybe that's why they all look so miserable. Ten people, and not a single one smiling."

Not a single one who looked like the woman in the painting, either — in this photo or in any of the others we'd seen. I
sighed and looked around at the other tables. A woman with
wispy hair held a magnifying glass over a yellowed paper. A
white-haired man with a beard was smiling in our direction.

"Hey, isn't that John the tour guide?" I waved, and he
made his way over to us.

"Doing some family research?" he asked. "I remember looking at this file myself some years ago, when I was
researching the neighborhood near the castle."

Zac introduced himself, and the two of them kept talking
while Hazeem and I flipped through the last few photos in
the file. Grumpy-looking women in long dresses. Snooty
men in suits. A marginally-happier woman with a bicycle in
a park. "Hey, look at this." I picked up a yellowed photo we
had just turned over. "The stamp on the back says Maynard's
Photographic Studio."

Hazeem looked at me blankly.

"Don't you remember?" I asked. "You gave me that book
about Hannah Maynard, one of the first female photographers in Canada, maybe in the world. She did all kinds of
crazy things with photos — stuff most people wouldn't try
until they could do it with computers a hundred years later.
There's this one where she's drinking tea with herself and

she's also in the framed picture above the table, slopping tea out of the frame."

The two adults had stopped talking. Zac was looking at me with raised eyebrows — he knew I was never much into photography, and I'd never mentioned this book to him — and John was smiling. "We have another budding local historian, I see."

Zac reached for the photo and flipped it over to show three people standing in front of our grandmother's house, frowning into the camera. "Nothing unusual here."

"What about this?" Hazeem picked up the last image in the folder. "There's definitely something weird about this one." Two parents and three kids, and the youngest was barely a toddler, sitting rigid in a chair.

"What's with his eyes?" I asked. "They look like someone drew them in."

"I remember this photo." John squinted at it for a moment. "Hard to forget it, really. I suspect the little fellow in the middle was no longer living when the photo was taken."

"What?!" I asked. "The kid dies, and they still went ahead with the photo shoot? What kind of weird family is this?"

"No," John said. "I should explain. They wouldn't have gone ahead *in spite* of the little fellow dying. They probably organized the photo session *because* he'd died. Cameras were expensive. Most families didn't have one and had never had their photos taken, so posing with the dead person was their last chance for a photo with them."

We all stared at the picture.

"At least for once there's a reason for them to look miserable," Zac said. "Those poor kids. Imagine your parents making you stand next to your dead brother for a photo right after he died."

"Maybe it was worth it," Hazeem said quietly. "Better than forgetting what he looked like, you know?"

I felt my stomach twist. We weren't talking about random people in a photo anymore. I knew Hazeem was thinking about his grandfather, and now I was thinking about losing Zac and what it would be like if we'd never had a single picture taken. Of course, I'd want one. "That little guy was so young."

"It feels weird to look at these people and not know who any of them are," Zac said, "even though we're related to them. Frida, any photos you want copies of?"

"For sure not this one." I already felt like it would be blazing on the back of my eyelids when I went to sleep that night. "Maybe one of the house?"

Zac flipped back through the file, found the first image, and headed for the information desk.

"So much for that," I said quietly to Hazeem.

"Were you looking for something specific?" asked John, who obviously had very good hearing.

"Uh, no. Not really." I couldn't tell him about the portrait when Zac might walk in on the conversation at any moment. "I was hoping we'd find a few happy pictures of our family. They were all so serious."

"That was fairly typical for the times. It seems to me ..." John tapped a finger over his lips. "Ah, yes! I once read an article about this. People didn't smile for photographs because aristocrats in painted portraits had always looked serious. Yet *that* was probably only because it would have been too much work to hold a smile for hours while an artist painted. Funny how traditions carry on, isn't it? I believe smiling for photographs didn't become common until the 1930s."

"So maybe they were a happy family after all," I said. For some reason, that felt like a relief.

Zac showed up, we said goodbye to John, and we checked out of the archives.

On our way home, I told my brother about the painting. "I wanted to find out who the woman was before I told you, though. We asked Anna, and I talked to Jennifer at the art gallery about the painter, J. Nille, remember?"

"I wondered what that was all about," Zac said and kept walking.

I stopped and stared at him. Hazeem stopped next to me, and Zac took a few seconds to realize we weren't beside him anymore. He turned and looked around, as though maybe he'd missed a rare bird flying past or a circus performer on the lawn. "What's up?"

"I'm telling you about a mysterious painting hidden in a secret panel in a desk drawer," I said, "and you don't even seem surprised." Or interested.

Zac rubbed a hand over his eyes. "Sorry, Frida. I don't mean to be a wet blanket. There's just so much mysterious stuff in that house. Money crammed into shoes. Pill bottles hidden in the potted plants. A stack of coupons for American cheese —I found those poking out of an air vent, the other day. Grandma must have been pretty far gone by the time she died. It makes me sad. I feel like we should have been there for her."

"How can you be there for someone who won't even talk to you?" I asked him and then turned to Hazeem before he got the wrong idea. "It wasn't like with your grandfather. He spent time with you. He was involved in your life. We wrote to our grandmother all the time. We called, but she never answered. She didn't want anything to do with us. Who knows why?"

Hazeem nodded, like he knew we weren't elder-haters. "I don't know anything about what old people like to hide, but this painting seems different from money stuffed in shoes."

"Yes," I said. "I'll show it to you when we get home, Zac. It's super-well done, and I'm not even sure Grandma knew about it. Clarence could have hidden it in the desk when he built it, right?"

"I guess so," Zac said. "I'm not sure we'll ever find out, though. It must be disappointing after all that research."

Seeing Zac's lack of curiosity was even more disappointing, but I wasn't about to kick him when he was down. We walked along in silence for a bit and eventually talked about other things.

After we said goodbye to Hazeem, I took the front steps two at a time, and as Zac got to the upstairs living room, I was already standing there with the painting. "Here. Have you seen this one before?"

My brother took it between his fingertips. "Never. I'd remember this face. She doesn't look as frowny as our other relatives. Maybe that's why Grandma kept it — the beloved non-snooty relative, as treasured as American cheese, money, and pill bottles."

I shook my head. "I still think Clarence hid it in the desk. That would explain why you never saw it."

"You can keep it, if you want," Zac said.

"Seriously?" I asked. "I thought for sure you'd try to sell it."

"I might have," he said, "but pricing art is a whole different ball game. If no one's ever heard of the artist, chances are it wouldn't go for much anyway."

"You're letting me have it because it's practically worthless then?" I teased. "Thanks a lot."

He rolled his eyes, but he was smiling too (finally). "It's worth a lot to you, so I'd rather you have it than some random stranger." He paused for a second. "Okay, and maybe if I let you keep it, I'll feel less bad about donating those other portraits before you were old enough to appreciate them."

"Stop!" Now that I knew I could keep this painting, I was ready to be more generous. "You ditched some dusty paintings of grumpy relatives, and you kept me. I'm good with that, and to be honest, once I saw those others, I couldn't imagine keeping them anyway. I like this one, though. No offense to Sophie Pemberton, but I don't think she had much to work with in her models. This woman actually looks like she could be friendly."

"Good to know there was at least one in our family," said Zac. "There's hope for future generations. Now how about some lunch?"

In my dream, the toddler walks into my bedroom. He is in black and white, like he was in the photo, wearing one of those old-fashioned poofy nighties that goes down to his ankles. Someone has drawn open eyes onto his closed lids. He toddles over to the stained-glass window, which is just his height. It's open, and he sticks his arm out and then his head, like he's going to dive out and free-fall into the backyard. I rush to him, as he slides out. I watch him fall, and right before his little body hits the ground —

I woke up with a start, kneeling next to the open window, my face pressed close to the opening as if I might see that tiny body lying on the ground beneath the cherry tree. *It was only a dream*, I told myself. *There is no toddler.*

The smell of cigarette smoke wafted in from somewhere outside. I peered out but couldn't see anyone. For a long time, I sat there, thinking about that little boy and how history might have been different if he had lived. He might have gone on to find a cure for cancer. Or maybe he would have been a mass murderer. Either way, the world could never be the same.

I shook my head. It was bad enough inventing alternate realities where my mother was alive. Was I going to do the same for relatives that died a hundred years ago too?

It took me a long time to fall back asleep.

Chapter Ten

"Welcome aboard!" Pierre swept his arm toward the cabin of his sailboat.

I hopped on deck with Zac right behind me. Pierre's little sailboat was one of my favorite places in the world: small, cozy, and totally Pierre. He'd spent twenty years building it in his front yard in Regina, a big city in the middle of a landlocked province, but by now, he'd lived in it for as long as I could remember.

"You are in luck," he said. "I have made the most incredible lavender lemonade ever to dance on your tongue. Would you like some?"

I gave him a hug that almost knocked him into the tiny cabin.

"*Attention!*" He laughed and hugged me back. "Come in, come in."

The entire boat, inside and out, was chocolate- and honey-colored wood, polished to a shine. His living space made our own tiny house look huge, and Pierre and I had to sit down to make room for Zac to duck into the cabin. "Looking good, Pierre," my brother said. "Shipshape, as usual, and new curtains, right?"

Pierre glowed and patted the door of a kitchen cupboard. "She is holding up well, this little boat. All those years when my neighbors thought I was crazy building it, but I got the last laugh, *unh*?"

"Couldn't really blame the neighbors, though, could you?" Zac teased. "Who spends twenty years building a boat in his front yard in Regina?"

"Oh, the same kind of person who would travel the world with a tiny little sister," Pierre said, handing Zac and me each a cold glass of lemonade, a cloth napkin, and a cookie. They always had this kind of conversation, comparing and celebrating each other's weirdness. "Sit down, sit down."

My brother and I squeezed in on one side of the table. Pierre updated us on his quest to find a new propeller (no luck yet). Zac told him about the buyer he'd found for the dusty old croquet set in the hall closet. "Turns out croquet is making a comeback, and people will pay ridiculous prices for authentic old sets."

"The mallets will probably disintegrate the second someone tries to hit a ball," I said.

"Buyer beware," said Zac.

"The neighbor across the street says she remembers —"

"How is Anna doing?" Pierre asked. "I always liked her."

A phone rang. "It is yours, my friend," Pierre told Zac. "I never turn my ringer on."

Zac patted himself down and eventually figured out that the sound was coming from his backpack. "Sorry. I have to take this. It might be about the desk."

I sighed. "He's obsessed with leasing it to someone as an art piece now. Ever since Liz turned him down, it's like his mission to find someone who proves that his price wasn't ridiculous after all."

"Well, good luck to him," Pierre said. "It is an enormous piece of furniture. He will need to find someone with a very, very big house."

"You mean you're not interested?" I teased and took a sip from my glass. "Hey, this lemonade is fantastic!"

"*Merci, merci!* Have some more." He refilled my glass. I was about to mention the portrait I'd found in the desk when he asked what I'd been drawing lately. "I still have in my bedroom your picture of the raven. I enjoy it every day."

I pulled my sketchbook from my bag to show him what I'd been working on — the Langham Court book exchange, the front of Hazeem's house, a view of the castle from the downstairs kitchen window, the outline of the spoons and teacups — and Pierre whistled. "You are indeed a talented artist. Your mother would have been very proud, Frida."

Something about the way he said it, and the fact that he had known her when she was young, made me feel like she was reaching out across the years and patting me on the back. It felt strange, but good too. "Thanks."

"You know," said Pierre, "when I first met her, she was the same age that you are now."

Every time we saw Pierre, he made some comment like that. Before, I'd always changed the topic as fast as I could. I didn't want to hear about this person who gave birth to me but that I would never get to know. Now that I'd spent weeks sorting through family history, though, hearing about my mother didn't seem so bad. In fact, it felt like I should be at least as interested in her teenage years as I'd been in the life of my grandmother (or in Clarence's, for that matter). "What was she like when she was my age?"

Pierre looked at me for a moment, but if he was shocked that I had asked a question instead of running for the next possible topic, his face didn't show it. "She loved books. We lived in a big, old house that was divided into apartments. I used to sit on the front steps, drinking lemonade in the summertime — plain lemonade. I did not yet know the wonders of lavender. She would come home from the library with a backpack full of books, and we would talk. She was the only young person in our building, and she was accustomed to being around adults. We had excellent conversations. I missed her when she left."

She would have loved all the book exchange boxes in Victoria, I bet, and I was about to say as much, when I thought of a question instead. "Do you know anything about her dad? Anna said he was a cook at a drive-in, but he didn't come with them to Victoria, so Anna doesn't know anything about him." (Funny, Zac doesn't know anything about *our* dads, either. Family tradition, maybe, this absent-dad thing?)

"I met him several times," Pierre said, "but I did not know him well. He was not home very much, and he … stayed in Regina. It wasn't a planned thing … the move, you know. One afternoon, your mother and I were sitting on the front steps, talking like always. Later that night, she banged on my door. She was crying, and she said that she and her mother were leaving. Forever. Immediately."

Zac poked his head through the door and squeezed inside. "Make it stop!"

"What?" I asked.

"The phone calls!" he said. "Someone's coming over this afternoon to see the desk, but I got another call too, from Liz."

"She has changed her mind about the desk?" Pierre asked. "Or she is still pestering you about 'professional help'?"

Zac sighed. "She offered me a steep discount on her services. She must be desperate."

I groaned, still not wanting anything to do with her but also kind of wishing *someone* would step in and do something about that houseful of stuff. Gone were the days when I wanted to look at and draw every family keepsake before Zac sold it. His overwhelm was contagious, and the whole thing was starting to feel like a never-ending project. His phone rang again. (At least this time he knew where it was, since he still had it in his hand.) "Sorry," he said as he climbed back out to the deck.

I turned back to Pierre. "You were saying our mom and her mom left Regina in a hurry."

"Oh, yes," said Pierre. "Your mother was very upset. I tried to calm her down. Her mother showed up, and a few minutes later, they were gone. That is the last time I ever saw her."

I frowned. "What do you mean? Did you write letters all those years before — you know — the accident?"

He shook his head. "I did not know where they went when they left. The Internet did not exist. But twelve years ago, I was living in Parksville. I saw her name in the newspaper. She was coming up-island to give a talk."

His words were cold water down my spine. My mother was on her way to Parksville to give that talk when her car crashed.

"When I first read the article, I thought maybe it was an art historian with the same name," Pierre said. "I had a friend who knew how to use the Internet, so he helped me to write to this art historian to ask. It was your mother, and she remembered me. We talked on the phone, and we planned to meet for supper after her presentation." He looked down at his hands.

I bet we were both thinking the same thing. *If it hadn't been for that presentation, if she'd stayed home that day —*

"I found out when the funeral was," Pierre said. "I went, and I met your brother for the first time."

Zac climbed back into the little kitchen. "And I was so charming that he knew he needed to bask in my grandeur, so he sold everything he owned in Parksville and moved here to look after us. As one does."

Pierre tossed a balled-up napkin at him. "Always a goof. I was ready for a change. You needed help. It all worked out."

As if life was that simple. You see something that needs doing, and you do it, even if it means looking after the two orphans of a neighbor you haven't seen in decades. It would sound far-fetched if you didn't know Pierre, but he didn't play by anyone else's rules. He was the one who encouraged Zac to move to Argentina with me and become a nanny, and he'd encouraged every one of our moves ever since. *Life is what you make of it* was a motto that he, and now Zac, always lived by.

For lunch, Pierre fried up prawns that a friend had caught earlier that morning, and then we all climbed out of the boat and walked up to Government Street to get ice cream. We were anything but an average family, but Zac always said you make your own luck, and I felt lucky that Pierre had come into our lives, no matter how weird it was that he did.

Chapter Eleven

"*The Magic of Jell-O!*" I held up a worn paperback. Hazeem and I had spent the whole afternoon pedaling around different neighborhoods, slipping Anna's unwanted mystery novels into book exchange boxes, taking from the overstuffed ones to give to the empty, like two modern-day, pedaling Robin Hoods. "You never know what you're going to find. This is the best title yet."

"Is it about Jell-O chemistry?" Hazeem tucked his book-box map into his pocket. "I should tell my science teacher. He's totally into recipes and why they work. Last year, we made a fake apple pie out of crackers — no apples, only crackers, cream of tartar, water, and sugar — and it was like eating real apple pie. The texture and the sour-sweet combination tricks your brain into thinking you're eating cooked fruit."

I laughed. "I love how you have a story for everything."

"It's because I write things down." He patted the note-pad that was always in his back pocket. "Every time I learn something interesting, I write it down and that helps me remember it better. Then I also notice more things because I'm always looking for something to write down. I wrote an article about that fake apple pie and sent it to a science magazine. I haven't heard yet whether they'll publish it, but I hope so. My mom says you never know until you try."

I nodded, impressed. No way was I ready to send my drawings to get published anywhere. "I hope they *do* publish it."

"Thanks."

I pulled out my sketchbook and flipped through drawings and random notes to the page starting with *The Art of Gift Wrapping*. "Speaking of writing things down, I'm going to write down this title." At the bottom of the list, I added *The Magic of Jell-O*. I couldn't imagine how I'd ever weave notes like these into a conversation, but I liked my list anyway. Sketchbooks were one thing my brother never made me get rid of. Someday I'd look back on this and remember the book exchanges I visited with Hazeem this summer.

"I'm thirsty," Hazeem said, "and I'm out of water."

"There's probably a fountain in the park," I said, "but are we close to the Inner Harbour here?"

"About five blocks away," he said. "Why?"

"Do you want to go visit Pierre?" I asked. "If he's home,

I bet he'll offer us some lavender lemonade. It's the best I've ever had."

The Inner Harbour was crawling with tourists. We parked our bikes at street level and took the steps down to the causeway, stopping every few feet because someone in front of us wanted to take a picture of the Empress Hotel or the Legislature buildings.

"At least the marina isn't so crowded," I said when we finally stepped onto the ramp down to the piers. "Lots of boats, but hardly any people. Pierre's is this way."

"Look that that one!" Hazeem pointed to a sleek white-and-black luxury yacht that took up the entire far end of the marina. "It's bigger than a house!"

"Three floors," I said. "Probably with a hot tub on top. Zac and I saw a boat like that in Greece. From a distance, of course. We were on a cliff overlooking it, and you could see all these security people walking around."

"This one's got cameras instead," said Hazeem. "One every few feet."

"Pierre's boat is down this way," I said, "in the poorer row." We walked to the end of that pier. I hopped aboard.

"I like this one better," Hazeem said. "You stepped aboard a full three seconds ago, and no bodyguards have finger-printed you yet."

I called for Pierre, but no one answered. The cabin door was locked too. "Sorry," I said. "I guess he's out, but I know there's a water fountain up on the causeway. I stopped there last time."

We went to refill our bottles and eventually swung back onto our bikes. "Hey, wanna go swimming sometime?" I asked. "Zac was telling me about a place called the Gorge. It's ocean water, but warmer because it's in an inlet. It used to be super-polluted when he was a kid, but it's all cleaned up now. There's a swimming dock and everything."

Hazeem was looking at me like I'd suggested dining on slugs, and he shook his head. "I don't swim. Mom's wanted me to learn for ages, but nuh-uh. Not my thing."

"You sure?" I asked. "I could teach you, if you want."

"No way. I'll stay on shore, thanks."

We pedaled past the Empress Hotel, taking a road along the edge of downtown. We stopped to check the bike map Zac had given me before we left and made our way past Beacon Hill Park, up through Cook Street Village, past the apartment blocks, and up to the mansions on the hill. We'd just turned onto our street below the castle when Anna called to us from her front porch. "Yoo hoo! I have something to show you!"

We ditched the bikes on her front lawn and climbed the steps to where she sat on her walker. From her pocket, she pulled a small, flat square, about the size of my palm. The edges were white cardboard, and the middle was made of thin, black-and-yellow, see-through plastic.

"What is it?" I asked.

"A slide," she said. "You can put it into a projector so the image shows up large on the wall, but it works equally well if you hold it up to the light."

I turned, closed one eye, and held the slide toward the sun, suddenly looking into a living room with an ugly, orange-flowered couch. A woman and a teenager stood awkwardly in front of it. I recognized them from other photos Zac had shown me. Gloria's arm was around my mother's shoulders. My mom glared tight-lipped at the camera, like an angry bird.

I handed the slide to Hazeem. "My mother and her mother. Thanks, Anna. I hadn't seen that one before."

"Look again," she said. "At the wall in the background."

Hazeem spotted it right away. "The portrait!"

I grabbed the slide back, and sure enough, the little painting on the wall was the one from the drawer. It was framed, though, in a simple wooden frame that made it look like a thrift-store find. "So the portrait *wasn't* hidden in the desk for a hundred years. This was probably only forty years ago or something, right?"

"I imagine," Anna said. "It must have been your grand-mother's birthday or some other special occasion. I was hardly ever in their house, and certainly not with a camera. Gloria was such a private person."

Hazeem scribbled something down in his notebook, all sleuth-like. "I guess Zac was right about it being your grand-mother, not Clarence, who hid the painting in the drawer."

I shook my head. "I still don't think so. The money and the pill bottles and the American cheese coupons were all stuffed in weird places. Whoever built the fake bottom for the drawer put a lot of thought into how to hide something."

"American cheese coupons?" Anna asked, and I explained about the odd things that Zac and I had been finding.

"Oh dear," said Anna. "She certainly struggled in the last years. I tried to help out as much as I could. It was hard to see her that way."

Hazeem flipped a page in his notebook. "Frida, what's your current theory, then? That it was Clarence who hid the painting in the first place, and then your grandmother took it out, framed it, hung it on the wall, and later put it back in the desk?"

I shrugged. "Who knows? But sure. Why not?"

"Why would she hide it again, though?" Hazeem asked.

"Maybe," Anna said, "she felt it was valuable. I do remember that she worried about things getting stolen when renters moved in upstairs."

"I still don't get it, though," I said. "How could it be valuable if no one's ever heard of J. Nille?"

"Maybe it was valuable for a different reason," Hazeem said. "What do they call it? Sentimental value?"

"Maybe." Either way, we were back at the beginning. No one knew who this woman was, or why she was in the drawer.

"You can have the slide if you like, Frida," Anna said finally. "Fancy me taking this picture all those years ago. I never imagined that someday I'd be looking at it with Gloria's granddaughter. Life does have its funny twists and turns."

She got that right. Weren't things supposed to make *more* sense, the more clues you had?

Chapter Twelve

Zac set a plate of kale salad and quinoa burgers in front of me in our empty upstairs kitchen.

"Why so smiley?" I asked. "You never look this excited about healthy food."

"Jennifer from the art gallery texted me," he said. "She invited me to an exhibit opening, as her guest."

"Oh?" He'd had girlfriends over the years, of course, but they never lasted more than a few months. When he woke up wanting to live in another country, they didn't follow us. Go figure. For a while, I was happy about that — I always knew that I came first — but these days, the idea of Zac having someone else to focus on was kind of a relief, and besides, I liked Jennifer.

My brother gave me a worried look. "Do you want me to ask … if you can join us?"

"No way!" I said. "I can look after myself for a few hours. I can see the exhibit another time."

"Sure?"

"Yes," I said. "Go. Have fun. Wow her with your knowledge of art. Oh, and you can tell her the story of the J. Nille painting, if you want. Turns out you may have been right about our grandmother hiding it, by the way." I told him about the slide. "Anna didn't think she'd seen the portrait before, but there it was in the slide she took. I can't blame her for not having noticed it, though. The frame was awful, and it looked like there was way too much tension in the room for anyone to be looking at the walls."

"Tension?" Zac asked.

I nodded. "Gloria had a big grin on her face, but Mom looked ready to explode, like they'd had a huge fight or something."

"If they hadn't yet, it was only minutes away, I'm sure," Zac said. "That's how it was between them."

"Really?" This was news to me. "Why did Mom live with her forever then, if they fought all the time?"

"It's complicated," he said.

I waited for him to continue, but he didn't. "Are you ever going to tell me *why* it's complicated, or are you just going to leave that hanging?"

"Some things are better left unsaid, Frida." He stuffed another forkful of salad into his mouth. "This kale is *so* fresh.

Totally worth going to the farmer's market for, right? Any requests for this weekend's visit?"

I sighed. "I don't want to talk about kale. You grew up knowing this stuff about Mom and our grandma, Zac. It feels weird that I don't know any of it, like I landed from another planet with no family history at all."

He stopped chewing and stared at me. "You're mad I didn't tell you that they fought all the time?"

"Annoyed maybe," I said. "Confused, for sure. Why hide it?"

"Would your life have been different if you knew?" he asked.

"You're not answering my question!" I said. "Is this why Gloria never talked to us? Because our mother had some kind of anger-management issues?"

Zac's eyebrows shot straight up. "No! That's not it at all!"

"Then what?"

He took a deep breath, put down his fork, and rested his elbows on the table. "Let me tell you what I think happened in that photo. If Gloria had a big grin on her face, then she'd probably already been drinking, and Mom knew what was coming. She was her mother's Chief Cook and Vomit Cleaner for a lot of years, Frida. It's not a bright chapter in our family history." His eyes locked on mine, the same look I give other people when I don't want them to ask any questions.

But I had to ask questions. In my mind, a pool of barf was forming beneath the painting in the slide. Anna had never hinted that Gloria was an alcoholic, only that she was "such a private person" and one who disappeared a lot, either to Hollywood or Regina or into her own apartment. Did Anna really not have a clue about the drinking, or was she trying to be polite?

"Now you know." Zac pushed his empty plate away and looked out the window.

"Well, at least things make more sense now," I said, "why she didn't help you after our parents died, and why she never wrote or called."

"I thought I was doing the right thing by not telling you," he said. "I wanted to give you a fresh start."

"Thanks." I tried to keep my voice gentle because he obviously didn't want to be talking about this at all. "It wasn't going to ruin my life to know I had an alcoholic grandmother, though."

"No, but I guess I wanted to erase it. Our mother spent her whole life picking up the pieces, complaining about it, and looking for signs that I'd be as messed up as everyone else in the family." He shook his head. "I remember the only time I came home smashed, Mom cried like I —"

"Wait. You came home drunk?" I'd never even seen him tipsy. He hardly touched alcohol.

"I'm human," he said. "I was experimenting. You'll experiment too, someday. But if you barf on the floor, you'll clean it up."

Blech. "You barfed on the floor?"

"Yup, and it was all crusty by the time I could see straight enough to use a mop." He gave me a half smile. "Look, I've read a lot about what's known as intergenerational trauma. Basically, it means that something horrible happens to a person — maybe they're abused, or they get raped, or they're in a war — and they don't know how to process the trauma, and they wind up passing it on."

This was sounding very woo-woo and un-Zac-like. "How does a person 'pass on' a trauma, exactly? Please don't say voodoo dolls."

"Come on, Frida," he said. "I'm being serious here, and I'm trying to answer your question of why I didn't tell you about Grandma."

"Fine."

"This is how someone explained it to me once," he said. "A psychologist. *My* psychologist. The one Pierre signed me up for after Mom died."

"You went to a psychologist?" This was an evening of many surprises.

"Yes," he said. "One of the best things I ever did. Anyway, this woman told me that when something awful happens, a lot of people run away from the pain. They try to block out the experience by distracting themselves — drinking, or overworking, or —"

"Buying a lifetime supply of ceramic raccoons?"

"Exactly," he said. "But none of that actually helps. It just makes it worse. The feelings get bigger and wind up exploding all over the place. That's how kids of traumatized parents can grow up to be traumatized adults, and the cycle repeats, from generation to generation, until someone stops it. That's what I wanted to do."

"That's why we left to go traveling?" I asked.

"Partly," he said. "Also because I'd always wanted to travel. I didn't want to lose you, and I didn't want to lose that dream, either. It was Pierre who told me to do both. Of course, I looked at him like he was an idiot because who travels the world with a toddler kid-sister? He crossed his arms and stuck out his chin — you know how he does — and asked me who builds a boat in his front yard in landlocked Regina."

I laughed. *That's* where that whole conversation had come from.

"His point was I could spend my whole life hating the rotten deal I'd gotten — like Mom did — or I could make the most of it. Maybe the only silver lining about not having parents is that you don't have to deal with them worrying that you're making a mistake. So I decided we'd see the world. And here we are." He held out his arms like a tour guide at the Taj Mahal. "In the house of splendors, with almost a decade of travels behind us. It's turned out pretty well so far, I'd say."

"Yup." I let out a breath I hadn't known I was holding. "Any other multi-generational, life-altering secrets you'd like to share?"

Zac considered for a moment. "Nope. That's it."

We cleared the table and slid the plates into the dishwasher. My mind was still buzzing. Only one thing seemed clear right now: Gloria could have hidden that painting in the drawer for a bunch of reasons. One night when she was drunk, she probably convinced herself it was worth a fortune and a renter was going to steal it from her. She still remembered the secret panel in the drawer where she'd found it in the first place, so she took the painting out of the frame and hid it again. By the time she was sober, she couldn't remember where she'd put it. So much for the big family mystery I'd imagined.

"Did you know that Gloria ran away to Hollywood when she was seventeen?" I blurted, more to get away from my own swirling thoughts than anything else.

"What?" Zac tossed me a damp dishcloth for the table.

"Anna told me. Gloria sent her postcards for years and then eventually showed up here again."

"Who knew?" Zac asked. "Does Anna still have the cards?"

"I could ask." This was the first time I'd ever heard him interested in something of Gloria's, maybe because it involved traveling. I finished wiping the table and tossed the cloth back to him. "Do you ever think how weird it is that, of our whole family, you and I are the only ones left?"

"Every day," he said.

"When we sell this place," I said, "it'll all be gone, all the stuff that connected us to them." Now that I knew what I knew, that was seeming less and less like a bad thing.

"Not our DNA," he said, "or the stories, and we can make the most of those. As for the other stuff, we won't have any belongings to hold us back, and enough money to move forward. That's the goal. That's making the most out of what we've got."

"We'll keep our little house, though, right?" I asked. "I mean, now that we'll have enough money to travel without worrying about how to make it, we'll still keep the house, right? I want to be from *somewhere*."

He looked at me for a few moments before he answered. "Yes, being from somewhere is good. You'll need somewhere to hang that painting."

I smiled. "And you'll need a permanent address so you don't scare off Jennifer with your constant traveling."

"That too," he said. "Now onward. Let's wash down this healthy supper with some ice cream sundaes."

Chapter Thirteen

"Take a look at these covers." Hazeem was kneeling next to an open cardboard box in Anna's living room when I arrived. It was a warm summer evening. Zac was off to the art gallery, and I'd promised to help sort the box of books Anna had found in a hall closet. "Nancy Drew and Hardy Boys. Every single cover is a painting. You'll love them, Frida."

"Would you like some tea, dear?" Anna asked. "I've made a lovely pot of chamomile, perfect for this time of day. Hazeem, you know where the mugs are, and you're so much quicker than I am these days. Would you mind — ?"

"No problem." Hazeem bounced up and went through to the kitchen. He was back a minute later with a teapot in one hand and three mugs in another, but suddenly he stopped and stared out the window. "What is *she* doing over there?"

I stood to look. "Isn't that Liz? Why is she looking into our windows?"

"Beats me," said Hazeem. "She just came out of your backyard."

Uh oh. Did she see the back window that Pierre hadn't been able to fix yet? He'd boarded up part of it, so it didn't look accessible, but those boards could come off easily if someone knew what they were doing, he said.

"I'm sure there's a logical explanation." Anna moved carefully across the living room and opened the window. "Yoo hoo! Liz!"

The other woman froze, but when she turned around, she'd stretched her face into a big smile and waved.

"Is there anything we can help you with?" Anna called to her. "Zac is out, but Frida is over here, if you'd like a word."

I cringed. Liz hurried down our front steps and across the road, her smile never faltering. "Lovely to see you all," she said when she met us on Anna's front porch. "Beautiful evening. I wanted to ask you something, Frida. You haven't by any chance found a … gold earring anywhere on your property, have you?"

I shook my head. "You think you lost it at our place?"

"I believe so," she said, "and it's rather precious. A family heirloom. I can't think where else I might have —"

"I haven't seen anything," I said, "and Zac hasn't mentioned it. You can text him, though."

"I did," she said, "but he didn't answer. I thought that if I could find it myself on your lawn ..."

"Of course, dear," Anna said. "I'm sorry about the earring, but I'm glad to hear you've given up harassing these young people about their grandmother's things." She locked eyes with the younger woman. "Now, would you like a nice cup of chamomile tea? I've got a fresh pot, and chamomile is wonderful for calming the nerves. You seem a bit ... het up."

"Oh, ha! Yes. Sorry about that. It's all a bit ... you know, worrying. I should head home. I ... thank you. See you later, then." She hurried off down the street, leaving us on the porch looking at each other.

"She's lying," Hazeem said as soon as Anna closed her apartment door behind us. "She wasn't looking for anything on the ground. She was looking up at the house. At the windows and door. Like she wanted to get in."

"Now, now," Anna said. "This isn't a Hardy Boys novel. This is Liz we're talking about, and yes, she's ... um ... rather intent on her work, but she *is* a neighbor, not some common criminal."

"But how else do we explain what just happened?" Hazeem asked and shot me a look. I shook my head as subtly as possible, hoping he'd know that meant *No, she doesn't know about the last break-in.*

"Anna," I said, "we should probably tell you that we were outside when Liz came over to talk about my grandmother's things. We were working on Hazeem's bike, and your window was open. We didn't mean to eavesdrop, but we kind of heard everything."

Anna frowned, but she looked more concerned than mad.

"It still doesn't make sense, though," Hazeem said. "What was Liz going to do? Bust down the door and carry out an antique stuffed chair?"

"Or a moose head?" I asked. "I'm sure she could get big bucks for that mangy old thing."

"Oh dear," said Anna laughing. "You two *do* have active imaginations!"

"Yup," I said. "Keeps life interesting. But it can be annoying too. Like I know for a fact that if I go home before Zac gets back tonight, every sound I hear is going to be Liz coming for the moose head. Do you mind if I stick around for a while, instead? Until Zac gets home?"

"Not at all, dear," said Anna. "You're welcome, and I don't blame you one bit."

"She came into the yard and was staring up at the house?" Zac was standing on Anna's front porch. The sun was about to set, and he'd arrived back from his evening with Jennifer with a happy smile that disappeared when we told him about Liz.

"Are you sure there wasn't anything else she was interested in, apart from the desk, the poker thingies, the classics, the clock, and I guess the spoons and the candlestick holder?" I asked.

"Not that I noticed," said Zac. "I kept hoping she'd spot a treasure and tell me it was worth a mint. She did give everything a good, long look, but not enough to make me think, *Watch out. This person's going to break in and steal a bunch of random stuff.* I'll go over there and ask her point-blank what's going on. If she mentions the earring again, I'll call her bluff."

"Do you want us to go too?" I hoped not, but I didn't want him going over alone, either. Liz's back cottage was far enough from the street that no one would be able to see what was going on there. I pictured her hiding with a baseball bat, ready to clobber Zac so she could steal whatever antique she had her eye on. Anna was right. I totally needed to calm down.

"Don't worry," Zac said. "I'm sure there's some logical explanation."

"Why does everyone keep saying that?" Hazeem asked.

We watched my brother stride down the street and disappear down her driveway. A minute later, he was coming out again. "No one home. I'll try again tomorrow."

"Goodnight then, I guess," Hazeem said. "If you need anything, you know where I live."

Zac and I crossed the street. He went up the front steps.

"Shouldn't we go in the back way?" I asked. That morning, we'd created a new sorting system, and now the front hall was so crammed that it was almost impossible to get through.

"Right," he said, coming back down the steps. "I forgot about the boxes."

"Once we're in there," I said, "let's check all the locks, doors, and windows. That woman is way too creepy."

We went around the back of the house, me sticking within a few feet of my brother at all times, even as he climbed the back steps.

"We're okay, you know," he said. "She's creepy, but you saw her leave, right?" He opened the back door slowly, as though someone might jump out at him at any moment.

We stepped inside. I peered up the dark stairway toward

our apartment. I could just make out the closed door in the gloom. The door to our grandmother's floor was ajar, though, and there was something else too. The smell of cigarette smoke. "Someone's been here."

"Don't panic," Zac whispered. "You stay out here."

"No way." I gripped his elbow. "Don't go in. Call the police."

He turned to say something but stopped when he caught the look on my face. Instead, he let out a long breath, stepped back outside, and pulled out his phone.

The police were there within minutes. Officer Kevin had a silver brush cut and a hooked nose. His colleague, Officer Brianna, was about my brother's age, her brown hair pulled back into a ponytail at the base of her neck. She was as friendly as Kevin was unsmiling. Anyway, Zac let them in the back door, they checked everything over, took our statements (including the bit about Liz poking around a few hours earlier), and asked us to come inside and tell them what was missing. "Sometimes it's obvious," Brianna explained. "A TV's gone from the wall, or a stereo cabinet is empty, but this place is … different."

Zac wiped a hand over his face. "You got that right."

"Can we go upstairs first?" I asked. "Everything I really care about is up there."

The officers shot each other a glance but didn't ask why I wanted to check on an apartment that only had sleeping mats, two lawn chairs, and a few bike bags in it. I dashed upstairs. The door was unlocked but shut tight. Inside, everything looked exactly as we'd left it, including the set of ceramic bells (in the shapes of dogs, cats, and squirrels in striped nightcaps) on the windowsill. They were staring at us like they couldn't believe all this was happening either. I raced to find my most precious things — the sketchbook, the art supplies, and the painting — as if random thieves had roamed the neighborhood scooping up colored pencils, white erasers, and family portraits. Everything was untouched —

— until we went downstairs again and stepped into our grandmother's kitchen. The window was wide open, of course, all of Pierre's camouflage gone.

"The rest of the silver spoons," Zac said, looking at the empty spot on the counter where they'd been a few hours before. "They were all packaged up, ready for a buyer in Flin Flon. I was going to send it tomorrow, with some serious tracking because that much silver is worth a fortune, but how could the thief have known that from looking at the package?"

"The wall clock!" I said. Above the sink, the faded orange-and-white wallpaper had a clock-sized circle that was brighter than the rest. "Who on earth would steal that ugly thing?"

"Ugly, but valuable," Zac told the officers. "One of those mid-century atomic starburst clocks, you know?"

They looked at him blankly for a few seconds. "Maybe it was like a trophy," the older officer said eventually. "Whoever was in here wasn't a professional. In through an unlocked window — you need to watch that sort of thing, sir, especially without an alarm system. They didn't make it past the kitchen, either. Chances are it was a young kid on a dare. He took the package and the clock just to prove to his buddies that he'd been in."

"The cigarette smoke," I said. "I smelled it in the backyard before. One night when I was awake, I smelled it coming in through the window."

"You did?" Zac asked.

I nodded.

"Common enough smell," Brianna said.

"I guess so."

They double-checked the house, pointed out places where we could "tighten security," as if we had any in the first place, and said they'd speak to Liz and a few of the neighbors and let us know if they found anything. "We probably won't, I'm afraid. I hope you had insurance."

Right. How do you insure a house full of mostly-worthless junk? With a window that doesn't completely close?

"Good luck getting to sleep tonight," I said when they'd left. Zac must have been thinking the same thing because after we'd barricaded the window with a cookie sheet, duct tape, and a potted plant, we went upstairs again, locked our apartment door, and pulled our sleeping mats, sleeping bags, and packs into the middle of the upstairs living room. Zac reminded me that it was probably a prank and no one would be stupid enough to hit the same house twice in one night. I guess he believed himself because seconds after we turned out the lights, I heard him snoring.

I tossed and turned, but every time I fell asleep, I jolted awake thinking I smelled cigarette smoke. Eventually I felt around on the floor for my flashlight and grabbed a book from the top of the art history stack I'd been building over the past few weeks. I burrowed deep into my sleeping bag to crowd out my own thoughts with cold, hard facts and someone else's voice.

Chapter Fourteen

O f all the stories I could possibly read before falling asleep, I wound up with a waiter in Europe who spent his free time stealing from little museums with bad security systems. He kept the tiny paintings and sculptures at his mom's house, and she thought he was buying them at auctions until he got caught stealing a bugle in Switzerland. By the time the police got to her place, she'd tossed a bunch of statues into the Rhine River and stuffed a pile of masterpieces down her garbage disposal. (She went to jail, of course.)

I woke up with my face mashed into the book, convinced that Liz was trying to break in to our house to steal a portrait by a completely unknown artist called J. Nille.

Right, I told myself. *Because somehow she knew that the painting existed, even though she'd never seen it before.* I rolled over to say good morning to Zac. He wasn't in his sleeping bag, which was zipped up and neatly smoothed, with his pillow aligned exactly the way he liked it. He'd left a note on the floor next to mine. *Good morning, Sleepy Head. Don't worry. I haven't been kidnapped by clock-and-spoon thieves. Got a payment from someone who wants Christmas kitsch. Rushing to send it before she comes to her senses and cancels the transaction. Getting some groceries too. Sorry about the table mess. I'll clean up when I get home.*

I was pouring myself a bowl of cereal when I heard Zac's phone buzz. I followed the sound to the kitchen table, which was a mess of brown parcel paper, tape, scissors, and the ceramic animals in nightcaps that the buyer hadn't wanted. Zac must have gotten a message and a bank transfer the second he posted the ad. It never happened like that. No wonder he dropped everything — including his phone — to race to the post office before the person bailed. Any moment now, he'd fly up our steps in a where's-my-phone panic, and he'd spot it under the squirrel, and we'd both laugh.

I froze, staring out toward Anna and Hazeem's house. I could see his mom wandering around the kitchen and Hazeem sitting down at the table next to the open window, but I wasn't really paying attention to that. Not yet. My thoughts had snagged on the idea of Zac's phone being here, and my brother being somewhere else.

Where was Zac's phone when he was showing Liz the desk? Did he have it on him? Or was it charging in the downstairs kitchen because he and I were both at a barbecue, and he figured he wouldn't need a screen for a few hours? Did it buzz while Liz was opening the desk drawers? Did he go look for it, giving her time to open the drawers, pull on the ribbon, and discover the painting? *Be reasonable,* I told myself. *It's a portrait of a dead relative, done by an artist no one's ever heard of. Who would risk a criminal record over that?*

But what if it *wasn't* by an artist no one had ever heard of? The canvas wasn't in pristine condition, after all. The discolored bit at the back showed that clearly. I ran to the living room, grabbed the painting, and stared at it. The corner where we'd read J. Nille was dark and kind of smudgy. What if some letters at the end of the signature had gotten erased?

I ran back to the kitchen window and threw it open. "Hazeem!"

He stuck his head out. "Good morning! We should string up some tin cans and a wire, like kids in the olden days. Maybe our adults would feel sorry for us and let us use their phones for once."

At any other moment, I would have laughed, but right then, I was too "het up." The more I thought about Liz and the portrait, the more I was convinced she was after it. Everything was too random otherwise: Liz wanting the desk and then changing her mind, Liz visiting Anna to talk about us and later poking around our yard, a break-in the same night. "Can you come over?"

"When?"

"Now?"

"Just a sec." He ducked back inside and then popped out to say yes. I grabbed the book with the painting in it and bolted down the stairs to the backyard and around the front of the house to wait for him on the porch. Being alone was the last thing I wanted right now.

Hazeem showed up with a backpack on. "I brought a few of the Hardy Boys to drop off at book boxes later, if you want … if you're not busy, that is. You … you look like something's up."

"Follow me." I led him around the back of the house. On the way up the stairs to our apartment, I filled him in on the break-in. "Zac and I both slept in the living room last night — freaked out — and this morning, I woke up convinced that Liz was after the painting."

We stepped into the upstairs living room, all the sleeping things still on the floor. Hazeem was staring at me wide-eyed. "Liz is after something, obviously. It has to be her, right? We totally caught her sneaking around the house, and break-ins never happen in this neighborhood. Mom checked before renting here."

"I think she wants the painting," I said.

He looked at me like maybe the stress had been getting to me.

"Seriously." Now that he was looking at me that way, I felt a little less sure about my art-theft theory, but I couldn't take it back now. I explained that maybe, the first time she came over to look at the desk, Zac's phone buzzed in the other room, and Zac went to find it, "That's when Liz could have opened the drawer, found the ribbon, pulled on it, and seen the portrait."

Hazeem frowned. "Okaaay, but why would she want to steal it? Unless she's really into portraits by artists nobody's ever heard of?"

"That's the thing," I said. "What if Liz knows something we don't? What if it's not J. Nille? That corner's dark and smudgy. Maybe the name had more letters in it, but they got lost in the shadows? Nillea, Nilleb, Nillec, Nilled, Nillee …"

He was frowning again. "I don't know a lot about painters, but none of those names sound famous to me."

"Not yet," I pulled out my sketchbook and a pencil. "Maybe it'll be easier if I write them down."

I added letters of the alphabet in a long column, and I'd just gotten to "Nillet" when Hazeem said, "Stop! That's a famous one, isn't it?"

"Nillet?" I asked. "I don't think so. *Millet* was, though. Jean-François Millet. He lived in France in the 1800s."

"And he did a painting that got stolen from the Montreal Museum of Fine Arts in 1972, right?" Hazeem looked ready to jump out of his skin.

"What?" I asked. "The Montreal Museum of Fine Arts? How do you know about these random bits of art history all of a sudden?"

"Pierre!" Hazeem said. "When I first met him, he asked about my notebook, and I told him about my writing and that I was working on an article about the Munich Olympics crisis. He remembered it, and he said it was so big that it bumped a lot of other huge news stories to the back page — like the biggest art heist in Canadian history!"

"Someone broke in to the Montreal Museum of Fine Arts and stole a Millet painting?"

"That and about thirty other pieces of artwork too," Hazeem said. "Pierre knew all about it. He said the thieves got in through a skylight, and the alarm system for the museum was down because it was under renovation or something."

"Seriously? Who deactivates an alarm system for —" I stopped. "Wait a minute. Pierre was telling you all about an art heist in Montreal and happened to mention one specific painting by Millet? Did he mention any of the other artists?"

"He mentioned a few names," Hazeem said. "I don't remember them now."

I shivered, a reflex that had nothing to do with the air temperature and everything to do with a new suspicion. "Pierre used to own a painted portrait and you're telling me that he knows a whole lot about this art heist ..."

"Tons! He was like an encyclopedia. Every question I asked, he had an answer for." Hazeem's eyes were growing ever wider, but suddenly he shook himself. "Okay. Let's stick to the facts. Fact one: Pierre knows a lot about the art heist, but that doesn't mean this painting is stolen *or* that he stole it. It could *still* be a portrait of a long-dead relative by an unknown artist."

"But why would someone hide it so well?" I asked. "If it was stolen, then the fake desk panel makes total sense."

"If Pierre stole the painting," Hazeem asked, "why would he hide it in your grandmother's desk of all places?"

"I don't think he did," I said. "Remember that it was on my grandmother's wall for a while, in the background of that slide that Anna showed us?"

"Right," Hazeem said. "So if this portrait belonged to your grandmother, then it probably has nothing to do with the one that Pierre had for a while."

"Oh," I said. "Right. So Pierre might have been involved

in the art heist and he had a stolen painting for a while, and this is a separate painting that my grandmother decided to hide in a secret panel in a desk."

We both fell silent.

"Have you done a reverse image search on the painting yet?" Hazeem asked.

I shook my head. "No. I was only interested in who the woman in the portrait was, remember, and the Internet couldn't — wait! Zac left his phone upstairs! If we do a reverse-image search, it might tell us if this is Millet's stolen portrait. That's something that might be online, right? Follow me!" I dashed back the way I'd come, with Hazeem right behind me.

Back in the upstairs living room, I placed the painting on the floor, grabbed the phone, took a picture, and uploaded it to the image-recognition site I'd seen my brother use a thousand times.

Immediately, the image shrunk to the top and the screen began to shift. Underneath I read *Best guess for this image: Jean-Francois Millet portrait.* Below that was a list of links. The first was a Wikipedia entry about the painter. The second said *Unsolved '72 Theft of Montreal Museum of Fine Arts: Millet's "Portrait of ..."*

"Go to that one," Hazeem said, poking the screen, faster

than I was ready for. It had been bad enough finding out that my grandmother was a mean drunk. If we found out that Pierre was somehow involved in the country's biggest art heist, I didn't think I'd ever recover. The portrait appeared on the screen, next to the caption *Jean-François Millet. French, 1814-75* Portrait de Madame Millet *Oil on canvas, 12 ⅜ by 10 ½ inches Miss Olive Hosmer Bequest, 1963.*

It was a perfect match. I clicked on the header, and the screen changed to an article about how the art heist went down. "*After midnight on September 4, 1972,*" I read, "*thieves climbed in through an open skylight. The skylight had been under repair. A plastic sheet kept the weather out. Unfortunately for the museum, it also stopped the alarm from working.*"

Hazeem groaned. "How does no one think about that in a museum with billions of dollars of artwork?"

I sighed.

"Never mind. Go on."

"*The thieves slid down a cord and tied up security guards. After selecting the jewelry and paintings that they would steal, the thieves used a guard's key to access the garage and steal the museum's truck. When they tripped an alarm, they fled on foot instead, discarding along the way 15 paintings, including a Picasso. Even so, they successfully stole 39 pieces of jewelry and*

18 paintings by artists like Rembrandt, Rubens, and Millet."

"This should be a movie," said Hazeem while I tried hard not to be thinking of Pierre in the starring role. "It says none of the art was ever found again."

"Until now," I said.

"What do we do?" Hazeem asked.

"We can't keep it." I gave him a quick rundown on the waiter/art thief and his mother. "She destroyed all that art because it was illegal to even own it. She wound up in jail anyway."

"Uh ... yeah," said Hazeem. "But you're not planning on shredding this portrait or drowning it in the Inner Harbour, are you? Someone stole this decades before you and your brother were even born, and how was either of you supposed to know that the house you inherited had a stolen painting in it?"

"Pierre." A lump had suddenly formed in my throat. If anyone found out that Pierre had been involved in the heist, he'd go to jail for sure. "What if he *was* involved in the heist somehow? If anyone finds out that ... Look, we just have to get the painting to the police. Right away. Anonymously. Okay?"

Hazeem nodded. "I get it ... but wait! What if Liz is an undercover cop?"

For a second, we both stopped breathing, but then I

burst out laughing. "She must be the worst undercover cop ever then, stumbling around people's front yards, getting so worked up that Anna has to offer her chamomile."

"I bet she recognized the painting," Hazeem said. "Auction house people must know these things. I bet she wants to resell it."

"It's probably worth even more since it was stolen," I said. "Like the Mona Lisa."

"Someone stole the Mona Lisa?" Hazeem asked. "Why didn't I hear about this!? I'm going to get back online after the summer's over and the whole world will have ch—"

"It was 1917," I said. "That's when it happened. Not now."

"Oh."

"My point is that the Mona Lisa wasn't even famous until it got stolen," I said. "But after that, people came from all over France to stare at the empty wall, and when the Louvre finally got the painting back, it was worth more than ever because it had this cool art heist story attached to it. Like this painting."

Hazeem peered closer at the portrait that was still lying on the floor. "Okay. So our facts are: One, Pierre knows a lot about the art heist; Two, this painting was stolen from the Montreal Museum of Fine Arts in 1972; Three, your grandmother had this painting on the wall at one time. Do you think she knew it was stolen?"

"No idea. How did she even wind up with it?" Alcoholics probably made lousy art thieves, right? And Mom was ... what? eleven? ... when the heist went down. She might have been useful in sliding through that skylight, but who brings an eleven-year-old on an art heist? Pierre wouldn't have, for sure. "All I know," I said, "is that we have to get this to the police. Fast. Before anyone suspects Pierre and before anyone else gets their hands on it."

Chapter Fifteen

Dear Police,
We think this is one of the paintings that went missing from the Montreal Museum of Fine Arts in 1972. We didn't steal it. We only found it. Just so you know, it's not our fault.
Sincerely,
Anonymous

It took us half an hour to write that, not because of the words, which we spelled out with letters clipped from old magazines — but because of the fingerprints.

"After all this work, we don't want to be tracked down and accused," Hazeem had said. "Because if they know it's us, and they figure out that we know Pierre ..."

"Right," I said. "But they won't have our fingerprints on file anyway because we've never done anything criminal."

"Better safe than sorry." He grabbed Zac's phone and started looking up how to completely erase a fingerprint from paper. Downstairs, the gong-doorbell sounded. Hazeem looked up from the screen. "You going to answer that?"

"Are you kidding?" I asked. "What if it's *her*? I'm not going to face that wacko without Zac here."

He shrugged and read aloud. "Cornstarch. You make a paste and blot the paper with it. If you don't have any, Anna might."

"No way. We're not blotting a bazillion-dollar nine-teenth-century painting with cornstarch paste," I said. "Do that to the letter and envelope, if you want, but leave the portrait alone."

"Bread then," he suggested. "Apparently if you rub the paper with bread, it'll pick up the oil and dirt left by fingerprints."

I took the phone back, but I couldn't find anything about the effects of bread on artwork. "Fine. Let's do it."

"Just not with Mom's bread," Hazeem said. "If any bits come off on the painting, they might analyze it and trace the starter back to the Yukon. After that, there wouldn't be much doubt about who turned in the painting, especially if they find Victoria wild yeast mixed in with the Yukon starter."

"I think you're overthinking this." I grabbed some store-bought bread from the counter. "Zac bought it on sale, and it tastes like fog. I'd rather use it on fingerprints than in a sandwich anyway."

Minutes later, Hazeem declared both our note and the painting safe and ready to go. I used a paper towel to pick them both up, slid them into the usual book, and put the book into the backpack, along with a water bottle and a box of cookies. I still hadn't eaten breakfast, and the thought of food right now made me sick, but I knew I'd get hungry eventually.

"Bring gloves," Hazeem said, "for when we take it out at the police station."

"I don't have gloves," I said. "Where is the police station, anyway? Could you look that up? And where are we going to leave the p—"

A loud crash from downstairs. I grabbed Hazeem's arm, and he looked at me, horrified, either by the crash or by me grabbing his arm or both.

I let go. "She's breaking in again! The downstairs kitchen window doesn't close properly. We covered it with a cookie sheet and a potted plant —"

"You mention this *now*?" he hissed. "Where do we go? Will she come up here? Why don't you have any furniture? Where do we *hide*?" He leapt up, tripped over Zac's sleeping mat, and crashed to the floor.

"You okay?"

"Yes," he said. "Guess she knows we're here now."

"So maybe she'll leave?"

Feet pounded up the steps toward us. "Okay, Frida, where is it?" Liz called over the pounding. "I know you've got it. I know your brother's not here. It's me and you now, and I'm done playing games."

"The fire escape. This way!" I slung the backpack over my shoulder, jumped over the sleeping mats, raced to Zac's room, and pushed open the window. "You go first. You good with heights?"

"I'll take heights over Liz any day." He scooted out the window and down the metal ladder.

I got out at the same moment that Liz appeared in the bedroom doorway. "*Get them!*"

Who was she shouting to? I didn't see anyone in the backyard, but there was that whiff of stale cigarette smoke again. "Run!" I called to Hazeem. He darted around the side of the house. I took off after him.

Heavy feet pounded behind me. I should have run right after Hazeem who was now slamming into his house, but then Liz appeared, and all I could think about was that maybe she'd nab me before I got across the street, and someone would call the police, and they'd find the painting in my backpack, and she'd sweet-talk the officers into charging us with possession of stolen goods, and Zac would wind up in jail, and I'd spend the next five years in foster homes.

So I dashed right. I ran as hard as I could until the pounding footfalls disappeared behind me. I kept glancing over my shoulder, and eventually I had to slow down because whoever built this ring road around the castle wasn't thinking about twenty-first-century teenagers running for their lives. This road would take me right back to where I'd started from, and who knew how long Liz and her thug friend would be lurking across the street?

I needed somewhere to hide, somewhere close enough to get back to Hazeem when the coast was clear. The sooner we got this painting to the police, the better, but I didn't know where the police station was, and Zac's phone was still on the floor by our sleeping mats. Hide. *Hide!* Where could I go that they would never think to look?

Liz's place. No way she'd look for me there, right? She'd expect me to stay as far away as possible.

I'd slowed to a fast walk now, checking behind me every few seconds, and peering ahead too, because I was almost all the way around the ring road. I could see Liz's hedge at the bend in front of me. I crouched down and peeped past the bushes toward Hazeem's house. It was almost a full block away. Liz and a big man stood on the sidewalk a few houses down, their backs to me and their heads bent together.

I backtracked a few feet, crossed the street on this side of the curve so they wouldn't see me, and I walked quickly, head down, toward the book box. Stepping into Liz's driveway, I tiptoed past the big bin full of roof bits and made it to the cottage. Back here, the hedge had been hacked within an inch of its life to make space for another dumpster, and behind *it* was a hole in the bushes big enough to squeeze through. It looked like someone's yard on the other side. I stared at what I could see through the hole for a few seconds. It looked perfectly safe if I needed to dart over there at any point.

Which was good, because suddenly I heard Liz's voice and the man's, coming toward me. "How could you let her take off like that?" Liz's voice was shrill. "She's the one who knows where it is. We can't search the whole house. We don't have that kind of time. I promised David the painting by tonight."

"Tell him there's been a delay," the man's voice said.

Liz made a strangled sound. "You don't know this guy. He gets what he wants, when he wants it. He pays well, but people who screw up face big consequences."

"You didn't catch her either," the man said. "She was faster than both of us."

"You're supposed to be the muscle here. That's what I hired you for." Her voice was only a few meters from me now. I heard her fumbling with keys. "I'm the one with my neck on the line. God, you have no idea."

"No idea, eh?" There was a new sound then. Like someone rustling something out of a pocket. Or a holster.

"You're not seriously going to threaten me with that, are you?" Liz asked. "I could have you put in jail so fast your head would spin."

"Ditto," he said. "Just trying to make my point, Liz. You hired me because I know some things. Remember that."

"For Pete's sake put that thing away, and don't even think about using it. David's enough trouble. We don't want the police involved too."

A click of a door opening, then closing. The voices were muffled now. I held my breath, my empty stomach lurching. I managed to wait for fifteen whole seconds before I hurled myself at the hole in the hedge and ran, flat out, across someone's backyard to the next street. I heard nothing behind me, and I kept running, the book bashing me in the back each time my foot hit the ground. I couldn't go back to Hazeem's now. What if I arrived on his front lawn just as they showed up on the sidewalk, waving a gun?

I needed to find the police station. But how? Ask someone? (That wouldn't be at all suspicious.) Go to the library to look it up? (Good luck keeping an eye out for thugs at the same time.) Dammit, why didn't I have a phone?

That's when I remembered Pierre.

Pierre had a phone.

Chapter Sixteen

That run to the Inner Harbour was the scariest of my life. Every sound or flash of movement was someone about to leap out at me. I got to the marina out of breath and sweaty, with a growing bruise on my back.

The causeway was almost empty — no cruise ships full of tourists around today. I slowed to normal human pace only when I stepped on the ramp down to the water. The luxury yacht was still there and so were most of the other boats, including Pierre's, thank goodness. *Please be home. Please be home.*

"*Bienvenue!*" he shouted from his deck. I hurried toward him, head down, not wanting to attract attention. He kept shouting about how gorgeous the day was. I could feel eyes on me from all around the marina.

I hopped onto the deck. I was panting, and my face radiated heat. "I was in the neighborhood and thought I'd drop by."

Pierre raised an eyebrow but only said, "Shall we sit on the deck? Such a beautiful day, *unh*?"

"No! I mean, yes, it's lovely, but could we please go inside? Now?" I glanced up at the walkway again where people wandered by as if we didn't exist. Phew.

"Whatever brought you here has you nervous, *unh*?" Inside the tiny cabin, he opened cupboards and pulled out plates. "Would you like some lunch? Or a snack? I have some seed crackers and a beautiful St. André. I have discovered an excellent cheese shop, not far from here. This one is a triple-crème soft cheese. You will love it."

I sat at the table, trying to slow down my breathing. I'd obviously lost Liz by now, I told myself, because otherwise she'd be on the deck, pounding on the door. I was safe, and so was the painting, nestled in my backpack, by my feet. In a few seconds, I would call Zac, and he would take over. I'd done everything I needed to do.

"Here we are." Pierre set the cheese and crackers and two glasses of bright red liquid on the table between us. "Cranberry juice. It is delicious with cheese, and Zac would never forgive me if I served you wine, no?"

I nodded and swallowed, my heart still beating too fast.

"Is … Is everything all right, Frida?"

"Yes. I mean, no."

He reached over to the counter to grab the jug of cranberry juice, never taking his eyes off me, waiting.

I didn't know where to start. "You remember the desk? Mom's desk?"

He nodded. "The huge one that Zac wants to lease."

"I found a painting in it," I said. "But it wasn't supposed to be there, and now someone's after it, and I'm running from —"

I wasn't making any sense, but Pierre had gone pale and was staring at me, wide-eyed. "Tell me about this painting."

"It's a portrait of a woman. It's about this big." I held out my hands to show him. "It was hidden in a secret compartment —"

He held his head in his hands and took a deep breath, in and out, before meeting my eyes. "So Gloria let her keep it. And you have found it after all these years."

I paused. Whatever I said next could shift the conversation entirely. I didn't want to accuse him of anything. "You know about this painting?"

"Wait." He slapped his hands down on the table. "Where is Zac? Does he know where you are? Does he know about the person who is chasing you?"

"No," I said. "That's why I came here. I need to phone him. To warn him. He left his phone at home, but he should be back by now, and he needs to know —"

"Here," Pierre said. "Call him quick. He needs to know that he is in danger."

"Danger? What danger?" I hadn't even told him about the guy with the gun. Did Pierre know something about Liz that I didn't?

"Call Zac," he said.

I picked up the phone and punched in the number. After seven rings, it went to voicemail. "Hi Zac, I'm at Pierre's. I need to talk to you right away. Please call back. He's got his phone on." I hung up. "He should be back by now."

"We must stay calm." Pierre looked like he was having trouble following his own advice. "Stay here. Eat some delicious cheese. Tell me about the painting, and we'll call again in a few minutes. I'm sure he will answer the next time. Or maybe he will phone us back before we call again."

"I can't tell you much else about the painting," I said. "When I found it, I thought it was some dead relative or someone my great-great-great-grandfather Clarence knew, but this morning, I took a picture of it to look up online, and it turns out the portrait was stolen."

"Yes," he said. "I know."

"What? How do you know?" I asked. "Why don't *you* tell me about the painting?"

"It belonged — as much as a stolen thing can belong to anyone — to your mother," he said. "I gave it to her before she left Regina."

I stared at him, hating the image of him forty-three years younger, dropping into the Montreal Museum of Fine Arts on a rope, snagging the portrait, and handing it over to a teenage version of my mother. "*You* gave it to her?" Who gives someone my age a stolen French oil painting?

"I was not thinking clearly. If I had thought about how I got it, I might have realized that it was stolen."

Oh, thank goodness. So he wasn't the thief.

"But at the time," he said, "all I could think about was your mother leaving. She stood at my door, crying. Gloria was behind her with two suitcases, saying they would take the next train to Moncton where her mother lay dying —"

"Wait," I said. "Moncton? I thought her mother was here in Victoria."

"You are correct," said Pierre. "Gloria did not want anyone to know where they were going. I did not know at the time that her husband — your grandfather — was involved with some suspicious people. He had disappeared, and Gloria must have been afraid that they would come after her and Kim too. She told me to sell anything left in their room and keep the money. That is when I remembered the portrait. Kim's father — your grandfather — had given it to me because he could not pay the rent."

I gave my head a shake. "Say that again? He gave you a stolen painting because —"

"I did not know it was stolen," he said.

"Seriously?" I asked. "My grandfather gave you a nineteenth-century French painting instead of rent — you never told me you were the landlord, by the way — then he took off and his family took off too, and that didn't seem a bit fishy to you?"

"Let me … explain about where we lived," he said. "It was a rooming house. Rent was cheap. I helped the landlord with chores, so that rent was even cheaper for me. I guess the old man liked me because when he died, I inherited the house. That was after your family moved in, and when your grandfather told me he could not pay the rent, I still remembered being in that embarrassing situation myself. He offered me the painting. He said it was a family heirloom —"

I snorted. "My granddad was a much better liar than me, obviously."

"It is true that you are a very bad liar, Frida," Pierre said. "I am happy about that. Your grandfather, however, was an excellent one, and I was very *naïf*. He said he was going away for work, and when he came back, he would have cash. In the meantime, I could sell the painting, if I needed to. I think he knew that I could never sell someone's family heirloom. Perhaps he thought that by giving it to me, both the painting and his family would be safe.

"In any case, the night your mother came to the door, I told Gloria that her husband had left the painting as collateral for the rent, and she could have it back now, since it was a family heirloom and they were leaving. Gloria was furious, and she did not want your mother to have it, but your mother refused to leave without something to remember her father by. They argued there in the hall until Gloria grabbed her by the arm, and they ran into the night, painting and all."

"You think Gloria knew the painting was stolen?" I asked.

"I am certain," he said. "She must have known the kind of activities her husband was involved in. I did not suspect until after he disappeared. When he gave me the painting, that was the last time I ever saw him."

"Do you mean that he took off … or that he was killed?" I probably didn't want to hear this, but I'd come this far. I might as well know the whole story.

"A few days after Kim and Gloria left, his body was found in a car on the opposite side of town. The police came to search the family's room, but they did not find anything because I had already given the stolen painting to your mother. What a going away gift — the very painting that had probably gotten her father killed and could have gotten her mother arrested. How could I have been so *naïf* to put her in that kind of danger?"

Good question, I thought, but I couldn't say that to someone who had dropped everything to live with me and Zac when we needed him.

"I tried to get in touch," he went on. "I wrote letters to everyone I knew, and I had eight friends in Moncton looking for her for months. When I learned that the painting was stolen from the Montreal Museum of —"

"How did you find out?" I asked.

"I had a friend on the police force. He was not allowed to tell me what the police were looking for when they came to our building that day, but I was so upset that he told me anyway. After that, I began to collect articles about the theft. I knew I owed your mother the whole story. I began to doubt that I would ever be able to tell her. But one day I saw her name in the newspaper in Parksville. It was proof that, no matter how stupid I had been about that painting, she'd survived, grown up, and become a respected professor."

"One who kept a stolen painting hidden in her desk drawer," I said.

He shrugged, a small smile on his face. "I suppose so. Although I imagine that she did not keep it simply because it was stolen. She kept it *even though* it was stolen. For her, perhaps it was a connection to her father, a souvenir from the time in her life when she had two parents."

A reminder of what life used to be and, in some alternate universe, what it could have continued to be, before everything fell apart. I could relate to that. "What did you do with the newspaper articles you saved?"

"I burned them when your mother died," he said. "Your brother had never heard of the painting. I knew I had to let it go. To focus on something more useful. You both needed someone, and I did too. I could not be there for your mother when her whole world was crumbling, but I could be there for you and Zac. It was good for all of us." He began to slice cheese again. "You know what you need to do with that painting now, *unh*?"

"Hazeem and I were about to take it to the police when Liz broke in to the house," I said. "Hazeem! I need to tell him I'm okay. But I don't have his mom's phone number. Or Anna's. Or anyone's."

"Shall we call your brother again?" He handed me the phone.

I dialed and the phone rang an agonizing five times before he picked up. "Pierre! Thank goodness you called. Frida is —"

"It's me," I said. "I'm at Pierre's. You didn't get my message?"

"I couldn't find my phone until just now!" His voice was panicked. "Are you okay? There's been another break-in. The police were here when I got home. Downstairs is a mess, and you were gone, and —"

"I'm okay." I wondered for a split second why Hazeem hadn't showed up to tell my brother what had happened, but then I remembered the painting in my backpack, and what would happen if we were caught with it. "Hazeem and I were upstairs when they got in. It was Liz and some guy. Are the police still there?"

"Yes," he said. "You need to come home and talk to them, tell them what you know. Is Hazeem with you? Does his mom know? She must be worried sick."

"Hazeem is at home," I said. "He's probably the one who called the police, but I can't come back just yet. Hey, can anyone else hear me right now?"

"No," he said. "The police are looking around. They checked up here first and when they couldn't find anything strange, they said I could come up and look for my phone to see if you'd called."

"Liz is after the painting." I explained about the reverse-image search and the art heist. "Hazeem and I were on the way to the police station when Liz and her friend got there. We got out, and Hazeem got home, but I took off because I had the painting with me. I came to Pierre's because I don't actually have a clue where the police station is."

"Hang tight," he said. "I'll talk to the police, explain the situation, and get to you as fast as I can."

"Don't tell them about the painting!" I said. "You could get arrested for having it. It's in the law or something that you can't own stolen stuff."

"But it's not our fault!" he said. "We inherited —"

"Pierre owned it for a while. Our grandfather — look. It's a long story, but *please* don't tell the police." I felt my eyes filling up. *Don't cry, don't cry, don't cry.* "I couldn't stand to have anything happen to you, or to Pierre. Meet me here at the boat, and we can go to the police station together."

"How do we explain to them about Liz breaking in, if we don't tell them what she was after?" he asked.

"I haven't figured that part out yet," I said. "Maybe if the police have the painting, and *then* we tell them we know who did the break-ins, no one can accuse us of anything."

"Frida," he said. "We haven't done anything wrong. No matter how messed-up our family was, no one can say it was our fault."

"I don't want you or Pierre to get in trouble. You're all I have. Please don't tell them."

"Frida, when I got back and I thought something had happened to you —" There was a choked silence. Zac cleared his throat. "Look, I won't tell the police for now. Just don't go anywhere until I get there, okay? I'll be there as soon as I can."

"And?" Pierre asked when I hung up.

"He'll meet us here," I said. "Then we'll go to the police."

"I cannot tell you," Pierre said, "how happy I will be when I know that the painting is back where it belongs, no danger to anyone."

I nodded.

"If you'll excuse me …" He got up and squeezed into the tiny bathroom off the kitchen. It had a door, but I could still hear everything, which was awkward. I stepped over to the cabin door and peeked out. Boats were moored all the way up and down the edges of the docks, but no one was out on deck anywhere. On the causeway, no one was looking in this direction. I stuck my whole head out and felt the warm sunshine on my face. It felt wonderful, but I couldn't stop thinking about what Pierre had said — about my grandfather disappearing because of this painting, and how we were in danger now too. The dude with the gun was scary enough, but Pierre made it sound like a much bigger operation than Liz and her friend. Who was David? And did he have anything to do with the people who had killed my grandfather? Would the same group that took my mother's father from her now be after me and Zac?

Chapter Seventeen

Something crawled slowly along the causeway. I looked closer. It was someone on a bike. A really old, red bicycle.

Hazeem! How on earth? I'd only just hung up with Zac, and no way could anyone pedal from Craigdarroch Castle to the Inner Harbour in a minute and a half. I watched him jerk to a stop, lock his bike to one of the posts, and hurry down the ramp toward the maze of boats.

I ducked back into the cabin. "Pierre, Hazeem's here! I'm going to meet him at the ramp." I was halfway out to the deck when the boat suddenly lurched. I spun around to see the untouched cranberry juice slosh onto the table right above my backpack, and I imagined poor Madame Millet's face dripping red. Without thinking, I grabbed my bag and slung it over my shoulder before climbing out into the sunshine.

Hazeem had darted toward the luxury yacht, probably remembering that Pierre's boat was somewhere nearby. I gave him a big arm wave, and when he spotted me, his face split into a grin.

"Luckiest. Guess. Ever," he said when I showed up in front of him. "So glad you're here."

"Well, done, Sherlock." I was about to ask how he'd figured out where I was when his gaze flew past my shoulder, and an alarmed look flashed across his face. I spun around in time to see a bicycle and its rider flying down the ramp, turning sharply toward us and screeching to a stop a few meters away. Liz jumped off, tossed her bike aside, and took three big steps toward us. "Hand it over, Frida. I know it's in your backpack."

"Forget it." I glanced down the pier to Pierre's boat, hoping he'd be on the deck by now. No luck.

Liz's jaw clenched and unclenched, her hands in fists by her side. The breeze tickled the back of my neck. A seagull called out overhead. Cars rushed along the road beyond the causeway. There was no one to call to for help.

"Hand. It. Over."

Hazeem pulled the notebook from his back pocket, cupping it in his hand like a phone. He poked his finger at it, like he was ready to dial. "The police are only a call away, you know," he said in a loud voice. He sounded strong, threatening even, which is why I didn't understand why he took a few steps backward, closer to the yacht. The second he did that, Liz stepped forward. Why were we backing ourselves into a corner like this?

Her eyes darted left and right, then narrowed at Hazeem. Her voice was a loud whisper. "Let me remind you that, at the moment, I'm the only one here who's not doing anything wrong. My hands are empty. Frida's backpack isn't. What would the police have to say about *that*?"

I swallowed hard, and judging by the smirk on Liz's face, she noticed. "I can offer you and your brother a deal, Frida. A long series of police investigations into how you came into possession of stolen artwork … or $50,000 cash and no need to worry about this painting ever again. Take your pick. I'm sure I know what your brother would prefer. Money seems pretty important to him."

"You don't know squat about my brother." My voice came out louder than I meant it to. "You think he's like you, but Zac knows art isn't about money. He knows this painting should be where lots of people can enjoy it, not hidden away in some private stolen collection." She rolled her eyes, and I ran toward her without thinking, but Hazeem grabbed my arm and yanked me back toward the yacht. The confidence in Liz's eyes flickered.

What would she have done if I'd run straight at her? Jump out of the way, or tackle me? Would she risk having my backpack (with me attached) fall into the harbour? How quickly would salt water destroy the painting, and would the Museum of Fine Arts still want it back, or — ?

Stop. I shook that last thought out of my head. I knew what I had to do — exactly what my mother should have done when she figured out the painting was hot. I didn't want it anymore. In fact, I wanted nothing to do with this whole weird family that tried to pay rent with stolen art, or made a secret panel to hide it for decades.

I flashed back to that alternate reality where the car crash had never happened. In this version, though, my mother was getting arrested for owning a stolen painting, and my grandmother was lying in a pool of vomit while I sat around upstairs in our empty apartment, and Zac lived in Japan.

"Let us through, Liz," I said, trying to sound way tougher than I felt.

She shook her head. "I'm not leaving without the portrait."

"She said," Hazeem said in a very loud voice, "that she's not leaving without the portrait that we're trying to return to the police. Did everyone hear that?"

I looked around and still saw no one. I stole a look at my friend. Was he cracking under the pressure?

He met my eyes and threw a look over at the yacht ... and

its many, many security cameras. I grinned. "Go wide," I whispered. He nodded.

"Onetwothree." We each ran on either side of her. She darted right, but I was ready for her and pushed her away … right into Hazeem who stumbled back and splashed into the water. Liz regained her footing and charged at me, but instead of pushing her away or escaping, I dodged and leapt across the dock to where I'd heard the splash.

I don't swim. Mom's wanted me to learn for ages, but nuh-uh. Not my thing.

"He can't swim!" I shouted and dove in after him. Hazeem came up spluttering just as I surfaced, gasping for air in the painfully cold, oily water. "Hold on! Stop thrashing and hold on to my shoulders!"

By this time, Liz was screaming "The painting! The painting!"

An icy feeling coursed through me that had nothing to do with water temperature. I still had my backpack on. Hazeem was panting and coughing next to me. I grabbed him by the chest and hauled him the few feet to the dock, where he could grab on to one of the tires underneath. "You're okay," I said, disentangling myself from the backpack straps.

"Nooooo!" Liz shouted as I shoved the pack farther below the surface. I kicked at it with my feet, silently thanking

Hazeem again for the book that had kept the painting safe and would now help sink it deep, deep into the silt at the bottom of the Inner Harbour.

Splash. I whipped my head around. Liz wasn't on the dock anymore. A few seconds later, she bobbed up, and as soon as she appeared, she disappeared again, hurling herself into the water below my feet.

"Let's go, Hazeem." I pulled myself out and gave him a hand up.

"The backpack!" he said. "Where is it?"

"Forget about it," I told him. "She can have it and all the trouble that comes with it. Let's get you warmed up."

Zac arrived without the police, like he promised he would. His knock on Pierre's door was so quiet that we almost didn't hear it. I could imagine him outside, looking around constantly, just like I had done only half an hour before.

"Come in!" I shouted because even though the painting was probably ruined and Liz had whatever was left, it felt good to make noise, to not be on the lookout, to know that, for the first time in over forty years, our family was free from all the danger that owning that painting had meant.

Zac poked his head in, and his eyebrows shot up. Hazeem and I were both sitting at the table, dressed in clothes that were way too big for us, drinking steaming mugs of peppermint tea. "Hazeem, you're here! What happened?"

"Let's just say we don't have to go to the police station anymore."

Zac's eyes flitted between our faces as I explained.

"All this while I was in the bathroom," Pierre said.

"And the good news," added Hazeem, "is that I think the whole thing was recorded on that fancy yacht's security cameras."

I laughed. "Yeah, Hazeem kept backing up and repeating everything Liz said at top volume. At first I thought he'd completely lost his mind, but it turns out he's a genius."

My brother looked impressed. "That was some quick thinking."

"Oh," I said, "and you should have seen him pretending the notebook in his pocket was a phone." I started laughing. Hazeem joined me, and soon we were all laughing so hard we could barely breathe.

Because our part in the story of that painting was done forever. Because we were free. Because we were all crammed into that tiny cabin — friends, family, whatever you wanted to call us — and it was exactly the way it was. For the first time all summer, I wasn't thinking of alternate realities. I was thinking only of what was actually in front of me, and *that* was spectacular.

Chapter Eighteen

We didn't see Liz again. The police officers said we probably wouldn't, either. Soon after they took our statements and saw the security footage, they had a warrant for her arrest.

No one showed up to work on her house anymore, and summer rain had poured into the half-done roof. I wondered where she'd gone (and who she worried about most, the police or David-the-angry-art-buyer). Jennifer had told me that some art specialists could fix up oil paintings that had been dunked in water, but ocean water would probably be a different story. Sometimes I almost felt bad for Liz.

Almost.

Mostly, I felt sorry for everyone who'd never get to see the *Portrait of Madame Millet*. I knew a bit more about the artist now because Jennifer had lent me a book. I liked that his family thought he'd become a farmer like them, and instead he became this world-famous artist who painted his wife, never knowing how many people would see that painting, try to buy it, steal it, or in my case, be completely confused by it.

It was like, whatever it meant to him when he painted it, the picture took on a whole different meaning each time someone new looked at it. I wondered if he sold it right away — maybe to pay for a new horse and carriage or whatever people bought in those days — or if he still had it after his wife died of tuberculosis. (See, I was right about the portrait-of-a-long-lost-love part. I just didn't know she was Millet's, and not Great-great-great-grandfather Clarence's.) I bet if dead folks can see what's happening on Earth, Millet and his wife had a blast watching everything that got triggered by that one canvas. Sometimes I imagined Mom hanging out with them and watching it all go down. Maybe her dad was there too, and Gloria, sober and peaceful, at last. It was a good picture.

The day after the painting wound up in the Inner Harbour, Zac hired a personal organizer. "It'll be worth every penny," he told me over supper that night. "If I'd found that painting first and tried to sell it online, I'd have been in jail right now. We'll still make a pile of money off the house and whatever we get to sell. We don't need to hoard every last penny."

"Hallelujah," I said, throwing my arms in the air. "I thought we'd spend the next ten years selling boxes of vintage paper clips and ceramic raccoons."

"It seemed like a good idea at the time," he said. "Yesterday jolted me back to my senses. I don't want to be like Liz, so desperate to make money for future travels that I forget to enjoy life now. Do you know that I can't remember the last time I went out to watch the sunset? What's the point of having extra cash if I'm missing out on real life while making it?"

I smiled. Zac was back.

We helped the organizer pack things into boxes. Some of it, she sold online for us. Other bits, we donated to the local Immigrant and Refugee Centre. By mid-September, my brother and I hopped back on our bicycles and pedaled to the ferry, leaving painters, roofers and carpenters to fix up the house. Jennifer came with us and stayed for the weekend in a little tent that she pitched outside our place. We pedaled all over our little island together, picking feral apples and the last of the blackberries. We roasted marshmallows in the fire pit outside at night, and we video-called Hazeem to tell each other welcome home.

Our grandmother's house sold in November, and we went back to see it one last time.

"That's that," Zac said as we walked away, "the last time any one of us crosses that threshold."

Jennifer slid an arm around his waist. "Congratulations, sir."

"I wonder if the new owner will keep finding ten-dollar bills," I said on our way down the wooden steps.

"Or world-famous, stolen paintings," Zac added. "Pizza for supper to celebrate? I found Mom's recipe a few weeks ago."

"You *kept* something?" I teased. "After all the lectures about letting go?"

"I didn't keep the recipe card. Just the recipe. Scanned it into my phone." He stuck out his tongue.

I turned to Jennifer. "*This* is what you've gotten yourself into."

She laughed. "Don't worry. I snatched the recipe cards from the recycling bin. I thought they'd make an interesting art project — you know, filed in a little wooden box, with annotations about whoever the recipe came from? It could be a piece about the science of homemaking or maybe ancestral knowledge."

"Conceptual art!" I grinned at Zac.

He rolled his eyes. "What have I gotten *myself* into?"

By then, we'd reached the sidewalk. Jennifer stood by her blue hatchback. Zac fished in his pocket for bike keys.

"First thing we should do with the money from the house?" I said. "Go to the Yukon to see Hazeem." He and I had talked almost every week since he left in September, and the more he told me about his life, the more I wanted to see it for myself.

"Not in winter, though, right?" Zac asked.

"Why not?" asked Jennifer. "It doesn't get more Yukony than January or February!"

Zac thought about that for a moment. "It's a good way to celebrate, I guess, going back to where our great-great-greats earned their money in the first place. It's like coming full circle."

I looked at Jennifer. If Zac's romance with her was going to work, some things needed to be tested. "Wanna join us?" I asked.

"Heck, yeah," she said. "I've got vacation time banked."

"You should keep her," I told Zac.

"That's the plan." He unlocked our bikes. "The other plan is pizza. Frida and I'll get the ingredients and meet you back at your place, Jen."

Jennifer drove away, and Zac took off like a huge house had been lifted from his shoulders. I pedaled more slowly, waving at Anna's window, even though I knew she was at the dentist this afternoon. (We'd seen her that morning, and she and I had been writing letters to each other before that, all old-fashioned with stamps and everything. I'd sent her drawings of our tiny house, of the forest, and of my bicycle. She'd written back with memories of my grandmother and news of what was going on along the street. No matter what Zac said, I was keeping those letters.) I stopped in at the book box, while my brother waited a few houses down. Well-stocked and tidy, but no art books, so I closed it up without taking anything.

"It's weird to be leaving it all behind," Zac said when I caught up with him.

"Thanks for letting me keep the desk," I said.

"Thanks for *not* keeping the stolen portrait."

"Meh. I wanted something a relative had made," I said, "not stolen, or hidden. Imagine if more of them had made things. Imagine growing up in a family of artists."

"No way would they have been able to afford that house."

"True." Even Van Gogh died super poor. He'd never have guessed that one day his paintings would sell for millions.

"Everything would have been different if they'd all been artists," said Zac. "We might not have landed on our little island, or traveled the world, or ever met Pierre, for that matter."

That thought hit me like sharp gravel. Much as I hated that my family was into stolen art, if it hadn't been for that,

Pierre wouldn't have been so obsessed about finding Mom. Or about looking after us when she was gone. Everything would have been different from how it was now.

And now, pedaling along with my brother, on our way home tomorrow and to the Yukon in a few months — now felt exactly as it needed to be.

We pulled up to the grocery store, bought what we wanted, and pedaled back to Jennifer's. While Zac cooked, she set up her laptop on Great-great-great-grandfather Clarence's desk to show me the website of an international youth art collective. "I'd be happy to write you a reference letter if you want to submit something." She looked at me with as much respect as she had when we first met, like I was a real artist, on my way to big things. "With your talent, you could definitely get in."

I grinned. Even if they weren't dating, I hoped they'd always be friends. Or that Jen and I stayed friends.

The evening flew by, and the next morning, before we left, I stood beside the desk one more time. "Thanks for hosting it," I told Jennifer. "And don't worry, I've checked the whole thing over for other stolen artwork. No Mona Lisas. No Rembrandts. No cans of poo hidden in a back panel. It's just Clarence's creation, pure and simple."

Phew.

Author's Note

Up for Grabs is a work of fiction based on an event that really happened. In 1972, thieves did enter the galleries of the Montreal Museum of Fine Arts, just as I described in this book. They stole eighteen paintings, none of which ever returned to the museum.

This fascinated me. How did the thieves choose which ones to steal, and what did they do with them after leaving the museum? Were they used in some kind of illegal trade, or did someone buy them for a private collection?

I began to read about art crime. I learned of people finding stolen artwork hidden away in barns, attics, or secret panels in walls. I wondered if any of the paintings from the 1972 Montreal art heist — Canada's biggest — might be hidden away somewhere, with younger generations of family members not even knowing they were there.

Thanks to the Internet, we can see images of the stolen paintings. I imagined that a young person who found Millet's

Portrait of Madame Millet tucked away in a drawer might think it was a dusty old picture of another dead relative. As soon as that thought entered my mind, *Up for Grabs* began to take shape.

With all my reading about art crime, I came across other true stories that I tried to tuck into my imagined one wherever possible. For example, the Mona Lisa really *was* stolen at the beginning of the twentieth century, and people really did go to the Louvre to stare at the empty wall where the painting had been. Another true story is the one about the waiter in Europe who stole art and whose mother tossed it into a garbage disposal and the nearest river when the police were after them.

I also tried to include details about artists in Victoria in the early twentieth century (when Frida's family members would have been getting their portraits done). Hannah Maynard was a photographer who practiced combining several photos into one, long before computers and photography apps existed. (Check out online her 1893 photo called *Tea time*. She put three separate images of herself in the same photo, and the result always makes me smile.) Sophie Pemberton was a prominent local painter at the time who really did study in Europe, win awards internationally, and then give up painting altogether because women of her social class weren't supposed to earn money. I thought she'd be the kind of person Frida's ancestors would choose to do their portraits.

Sometimes, I included facts but changed them slightly to suit the story. For example, at the time of writing, it's true that Victoria is home to over three hundred book exchange boxes, and by the time you read this, there may be hundreds more. In 2015, when *Up for Grabs* takes place, that trend was only just beginning, but I love those boxes so much that I just had to celebrate them in this book!

I liked the idea of Frida choosing to give back the painting (even if it didn't end up as she intended) and telling its story instead. After all, stories really can be the best family heirlooms.

Acknowledgments

Phew! I began writing this book eight years before it was published. In that time, both of my parents died, as well as my aunt and one of my dearest friends. I'd like to say a huge thank you to all my friends who propped me up during those difficult years, especially Susannah Adams, Chris Adams, Susan Braley, Ev Brown, Gastón Castaño, Farheen HaQ, Stacey Horton, Jenny Jaeckel, Betty and Bob McInnes, Mo Parker, Karen Poggi, Marjory Reitsma-Street, Jean and Gordon Sonmor, Mark Weston, and Allison Yauk. You've all helped make this book possible.

Thank you to Chris Adams and John Adams of Discover the Past Walking Tours for help with local Victoria history and for tireless fact-checking. (Any mistakes are mine alone.) Thanks to Stephen Topfer for welcoming me into the Art Gallery of Greater Victoria and sharing some of its lesser-known tales. Thank you, Rhonda and Julian Stark, for helping me break Pierre's boat in just the right place to get him stuck in the harbor for a while, and a big shout-out to Alex Castaño for plot feedback that made this a much better story.

I'm grateful to Mahtab Narsimhan who generously read my manuscript (twice!) and offered spot-on suggestions. Many thanks to my agent, Amy Tompkins, who found the story a home; to Barry Jowett, editor extraordinaire; and to the whole DCB team. Thank you, as well, to Julie McLaughlin for another amazing cover. It's such an honour to work with this incredible team of professionals.

To all my ancestors who got me to this point, and to my living family, thank you.

And thank *you*, dear reader, for allowing this story to become part of yours.

Michelle Mulder is an award-winning author of many books for children, including *The Vegetable Museum, Home Sweet Neighbourhood,* and *Every Last Drop.* When not writing, Michelle loves hanging out in the woods, making baskets out of found materials, drawing, diving into lakes, and diving into a good book. They live in Victoria, British Columbia.

I wrote this story on the unceded lands of the Songhees and Esquimalt Nations. There are currently 900+ members of the Songhees and Esquimalt Nations, and there is one first-language ləkʼwəŋiʔnə speaker left. I honor and recognize the countless sacrifices that they have made so that I may live in privilege here.

— Michelle Mulder

We acknowledge the sacred land on which Cormorant Books operates. It has been a site of human activity for 15,000 years. This land is the territory of the Huron-Wendat and Petun First Nations, the Seneca, and most recently, the Mississaugas of the Credit River. The territory was the subject of the Dish With One Spoon Wampum Belt Covenant, an agreement between the Iroquois Confederacy and Confederacy of the Ojibway and allied nations to peaceably share and steward the resources around the Great Lakes. Today, the meeting place of Toronto is still home to many Indigenous people from across Turtle Island. We are grateful to have the opportunity to work in the community, on this territory.

We are also mindful of broken covenants and the need to strive to make right with all our relations.